THE LUTE AND THE SCARS

THE LUTE AND THE SCARS

DANILO KIŠ

Preface by Adam Thirlwell

Translated and with an Afterword by John K. Cox

DALKEY ARCHIVE PRESS
CHAMPAIGN • DUBLIN • LONDON

Originally published in Serbian as *Lauta i Ožiljci*, by BIGZ, Belgrade, 1994

Lauta i Ožiljci by Danilo Kiš © Librairie Arthème Fayard and Danilo Kiš Estate

Translation and afterword copyright © 2012 by John K. Cox

Library of Congress Cataloging-in-Publication Data

Kiš, Danilo, 1935-1989.
[Lauta i ožiljci. English]
The lute and the scars / Danilo Kiš ; preface by Adam Thirlwell ; translated and with an introduction by John K. Cox. -- 1st ed.
p. cm.
"Originally published in Serbian as Lauta i Oziljci, by BIG2, Belgrade, 1994"--T.p. verso.
ISBN 978-1-56478-735-4 (pbk. : acid-free paper)
I. Thirlwell, Adam, 1978- II. Cox, John K., 1964- III. Title.
PG1419.21.I8L3813 2012
891.8'2354--dc23

2012015154

This translation has been published with the financial report of the Serbian Ministry of Culture

Supported using public funding by the National Lottery through Arts Council England

Partially funded by grants from the National Endowment for the Arts, a federal agency, and the Illinois Arts Council, a state agency

www.dalkeyarchive.com

Cover: design and composition by Mikhail Iliatov

Printed on permanent/durable acid-free paper and bound in the United States of America

CONTENTS

PREFACE

FOR DANILO KIŠ

1

There are various ways of imagining a new era of world literature. My favorite is to remember the story of Danilo Kiš.

His outside story is the devastated history of Central Europe. He was born in 1935. In 1944, his father, who was Jewish, was taken to Auschwitz, and did not return. In 1947, Kiš was repatriated with his mother to Montenegro, where he studied art, then the violin, and finally entered the University of Belgrade in the Department of Comparative Literature. He would go on to teach Serbo-Croat to students in various French universities, and he eventually settled in Paris—an emigrant in the self-imposed style of James Joyce. He died in Paris in 1989, when he was only fifty-four. But the inside story, the story of his art, is even more unique.

Can I put it in a highspeed sentence? His style was encyclopedia entries, definitions in historical dictionaries, legends told in footnotes, postscripts incorporating unsubstantiated rumor. His fictions very rarely looked like fictions. Instead, they adopted the look of annals or chronicles or pulp fictions. Because this, after all, is what happens to a life: if it's remembered at all, it's remembered in words. And this is the essence of the style called Danilo Kiš: it is always an experiment with foreshortening.

And if his chronicler wanted to recount an exhaustive prehistory of this style, then traces could be found, sure enough, in Isaac Babel, and Dostoyevsky, as well as in Edgar Allan Poe. But the real precursor was Jorge Luis Borges. In Buenos Aires, in his fictions written in the first half of the twentieth century, Borges invented a way of writing stories by not, in fact, writing them at all. Instead, he described them in antiquarian summaries, as if these fictions were already written, already part of a minute literary history: in fake entries from catalogues or encyclopedias. In his essays and his interviews, Kiš kept offering up new definitions of Borges's radical invention. It was, he said once, a

> new way of using "documents." It enabled him to compress his material to the maximum, which is, after all, the ideal of narrative art. I repeat: the document is the surest way to make a story seem both convincing and true, and what is literature for if not to convince us of the truth of what it tells, of the writer's literary fantasies. Such is the direction Borges's investigations take, and

they lead him to the pinnacle of narrative art and technique.*

Or sometimes he put it like this, in the language of logic: "The story . . . which emphasized detail and created its mythologemic field by means of induction, underwent a magic, revolutionary transformation in Borges: Borges introduced deduction . . ." For this kink introduced by Borges into the normal order of a story was a liberation machine, an ejector seat. It allowed Kiš to ignore so many of the old-fashioned problems, like character and psychology—all the otiose mechanics of *verismo*. I mean: you could make a Kiš anthology of irritation at the previous deadend methods:

Example 1
"What I can't stand is the serialized or *feuilleton*-type fiction of the nineteenth and twentieth centuries and its hidden omniscient author . . ."

Example 2
". . . the omniscience of the narrator and the art of psychological portraiture, those most pernicious and persistent of literary conventions."

---

*Save where indicated by the text, this and other quotes in the Preface are from *Homo Poeticus: Essays and Interviews*. ed. Susan Sontag, (New York: Farrar, Strauss, and Giroux, 1995).

But the history of world literature isn't a history of repeats. The Borges system was a gorgeous thing, but Kiš invented his own kink in that tradition too. For Borges's stories are inventions from the innocent half of the twentieth century. Whereas Kiš came in the aftermath. The entropic centre of his electric fictions is the century's twin death camps: the camps of the Nazi régime, and the camps of the Soviet régime. All history is crime, in Kiš's fiction. (No wonder he wrote a great, sympathetic essay on the fictions of the Marquis de Sade.) Borges had called one of his books *A Universal History of Infamy*, but his idea of infamy was so much more minor than anything Kiš knew: it was barrio gangsters and pistolets. So that where Borges's stories were really always investigations of metaphysics, wrote Kiš, he himself investigated the violent networks of commissars and *kommandants*. He used the document method to investigate history: "man's soul having long since been given up to the Devil."

His impatience with the usual psychological novel, in other words, was part of a deeper investigation. "Confronting imaginary characters with psychology is to my mind anachronistic . . ." Well, sure! It had been taken over by what Kiš called *schizopsychology*— the mass and murderous neuroses.

> Hiroshima is the focal point of that fantastic world, whose contours could first be discerned at about the time of the First World War, when the horror of secret societies began to come to life in the

form of mass ritual sacrifices on the al-
tar of ideology, the golden calf, religion
. . . I say "secret societies" because I am
speaking of the occult . . .

History is a history of violence. It always ends up as a garbage
heap. And so, in response, literature has to itemise and restore the
garbage. This was Kiš's wisdom. He once imagined a story that
would be a description of a trash can (just as Calvino—another
student of the Borges system—would try in his own late essay on
garbage.) "I believe that literature must correct History," wrote Kiš.
Its job, in other words, was the restoration of corrupted texts.

2

In Kiš's early fiction (*Garden, Ashes*, or *Early Sorrows*) he invented
his first method of restoration—a kind of luminous autobiography, in the magical imploded first-person voice of a child. This
voice is only foreground, an encrusted surface of detail that won't
give—but it gives everywhere—onto the catastrophic history un-
derneath. It is total indirection.

And this indirection is one of Kiš's most savage innovations.
You don't know what *showing* means, I think, until you've read
his stories. This kind of indirection might have been the professed
nineteenth-century ideal, a prim dislike of telling, but Kiš's indirection is more wayout and final than, say, the grand fictions of

Henry James. It was the only way he could find to encompass his vast material. For "to name is to diminish." Only by concealing a theme can you approach its total description. And so the reader is slowed into stillness by the density of detail in his prose—always about to transform itself into a list. I mean: you could make another anthology out of Kiš's love of the list:

Example 1
"This non-alphabetic enumeration, the onomasticon, is the system perhaps best suited to reflect the chaotic crisscross of *the prose of the world*, the magma that verbal mechanics merely *seems* to set in order . . ."

Example 2
"Reading the Bible, Homer, or Rabelais, I keep finding devices engendered by the disparity and incongruity of objects in chance encounter."

Which is another way of saying that the detail in Kiš is part of his new deductive method, it's based on his deep principle of collage—not the dead inductive methods of previous fiction. And this is why, in the '70s, when Borges was translated into Serbo-Croat for the first time, it was possible for Kiš to develop a new technique out of the old one. And so, in his great books from the

1970s, *Hourglass* and *A Tomb for Boris Davidovich*, he moved from the first person to the third person. In *Hourglass*, this created the intricacy of its form: where alternating manuscripts are finally endstopped by a single document: a letter dated April 5, 1942. In *A Tomb for Boris Davidovich*, this created the delicate juxtapositions of his stories about the Stalinist machine: their principle of thematic germination. His technique of the legend became complicated by the technique of the document.

3

Kiš's unit was always very small. It was a manuscript, or legend: a brief life. Then he'd organise these brief lives into collage compositions—novels, or story cycles, or cycles of novels. By the last decade of his life, his stories were adding up to a scattered conspectus of the world's crimes. The last book he published, *The Encyclopedia of the Dead*, came out in 1983. In a postscript, he described its theme: "All the stories in this book, to a greater or lesser extent, come under the sign of a theme I would call metaphysical: ever since the Gilgamesh epic, death has been one of the obsessive themes of literature."

But there was an entire studio of other stories—which approached this theme more secretly, more tangentially. These stories, collected as *The Lute and the Scars*, are the final products of his factory for restoring lost lives. And in their delicate state, they therefore offer the most vulnerable version of Kiš's art. The reader of this archive encounters all of Kiš's acrobatics—his fake documents, true stories, the fantastical everyday: all his methods to keep trying to restore the dead to life. In "The Debt," a life story emerges from a dying man's hallucinated list of debts:

> To Mr. Dinko Lukšić from Sutivan, whose hospitality made my days more pleasant and improved my health so that I could complete my volume of poetry: two crowns.
>
> To the young investigating magistrate, a Viennese, who, on the occasion of my arrest in Split, allowed me to send for my personal effects, which had remained behind in my pension; he brought me Kierkegaard's *Either/Or*, and that book would end up having a decisive impact on my intellect: two crowns.

In "The Stateless One," it emerges through a prophecy; in "The Marathon Runner and the Race Official," through a dream; in "The Poet," through a legend. These stories, in other words, are a primer in the method of Danilo Kiš. They will make the reader Kišified. And so eventually this newly Kišified reader will note even smaller acts of restoration: like the smuggled list in the postscript to the story called "Jurij Golec," where in the guise of describing a collection of furs, in order to just wearily prove an authorial point of *verismo*, his story becomes an arctic forest: "mink, silver fox, arctic fox, lynx, Canadian wolf, astrakhan, beaver, nutria, marmot, muskrat, coyote . . ." Even a postscript is another way for Kiš to create truths, not fictions. Because, as he writes, in another list, created by the list of animals, these furs have now "found their way into the story through the back door, after the fact, unleashing new sensations, opening new worlds: *métiers*, market forces, money, adventure, hunting, weapons, knives, traps, blood, animal anatomy, zoology, far-off exotic regions, nocturnal animal noises, Lafontaine's fables . . ." Yes, writes Kiš, with careful irony, at the end of the end of this short story: "great are the temptations of a tale. In contrast to a novel, however, one may not, in a tale, open the doors of cabinets with impunity."

4

So maybe I can put it like this. These exposed last stories from his studio prove that metafictional problems are in fact the ethical problems of history. They are different aspects of a single question: how do you restore the murdered to life? This is the deep question of Kiš's fiction, and it's one reason why his fiction represents an ongoing and future laboratory. His stories offer innovative, zigzagging ways of convincing a reader that a story is true. Why should there be a single method? He himself, as he recorded in an interview in 1976, with blunt technical clarity, had originally relied on the magical methods of the first person:

What I mean is that spells, incantations, charges (in Valéry's sense) were the only literary means I had to win over my readers, convince them that the words they were reading were not mere idle fantasies but a form of truth and experience.

But then there was a shift.

In *Hourglass*, where I switch to the third person and therefore lose the confessional tone, I was forced to use other devices (objective images, invented footnotes, "documents") so as to make readers believe, again, that they were reading more than fantasies or figments of the imagination, that they were reading the truth, *and not only artistic truth.*

And he added: "Call it commitment if you like: an enlargement of the circle of reality as well as an increase in the obligations resulting from it . . ."

5

Yes, there are various ways of imagining a future world literature.

And one of the most precious and wildest examples is the method of Danilo Kiš: this attempt to write minute encyclopaedias.

"I believe," he wrote, "that in its ideal, unattainable, Platonic form the novel should resemble an encyclopedia entry or, rather, a series of entries branching out in all directions yet condensed." A novel, in other words, should organise the maximum content in the minimum space. And it makes me think of the strangest text in *The Lute and the Scars*: just called "A and B." It's only a description of Kiš's most magical place, followed by a description of his worst. The worst place—Text B—is a village hut, described in his manner of deep detail:

> The walls have been whitewashed with an ochre-colored preparation made by dissolving clay in lukewarm water. The effects of dampness and sunshine are such that this coating blisters or develops cracks that look like scales or the faded canvases of Old Masters. The floor is also of pounded clay that lies several centimeters lower than the surface of the yard. On humid days the clay smells of urine. (A shed for animals once stood here.)

Whereas his magical place—Text A—is a place of total openness: a view of the sea from the mountains.

And you have to know for certain that your father traveled this same stretch of road, either on a bus or in a taxi he had hired in Kotor, and you have to be convinced that he beheld this same sight: the sun popping into view in the west from behind clouds that looked like a herd of white elephants; the high mountains dissolving in mist; the inky dark blue of the water in the bay; the city at the foot of the mountains . . .

But then this story or memoir or fragment ends with a postscript in a single sentence: "Texts A and B are connected to each other by mysterious bonds."

And with that sketched sentence, I think, Kiš transforms his twin fragments into the smallest novel possible: a universal history of loss—described without psychology, or character, in a couple of pages.

There are various way of imagining a future world literature. And one of them, I just mean, is to realise that Danilo Kiš is there already.

ADAM THIRLWELL, 2012

THE LUTE AND THE SCARS

THE STATELESS ONE

1

"He arrived in Paris on May 28, 1928."

He took a room in a hotel in the Latin Quarter, close to the Odéon. This particular hotel filled him with melancholy thoughts, and in the evenings, when he'd turn off the lamp above his nightstand, he had visions of phantoms with long hotel sheets fluttering around them like winding cloths. One of these phantom couples was familiar to him, and our man without a fatherland refreshed the image in his mind of the poet and his lover as he had seen them once in a photograph in that poet's scrapbook: she, Leda, with the enormous hat shading her face as if a veil were draped over her eyes, although it was a shadow that nonetheless failed to conceal the quiver of the years, barely visible, and of a certain sensuality starting to register around the lips; he, the poet afflicted with love and illness, his eyes bulging from Graves' disease but still glowing with fire like the eyes of a Roma master violinist. That Leda's troubadour had once lodged in this same hotel was a fact probably known only to the stateless one. Upon his arrival he asked the porter if a certain poet had stayed in the hotel around 1910 . . . and he mentioned him by name. The young man, obviously confused by the foreign-sounding name, blurted out in his mother tongue: "*No comprendo, señor.*" This proved to the stateless one yet again how irrevocably borders divide our world, and to what degree language is a person's only real home. But, taking his key in his hand, he was already heading for his room on the third floor, on foot, half running up the stairs, because he had been steering clear of elevators of late.

2

"The eyewitness accounts of the last period of his life are contradictory. Some see him beset by anxiety, avoiding elevators and automobiles with suspicion and horror, while others . . ."

Once, more than twenty years ago, he had read in the newspaper that a young man in Pest plummeted into a basement on board an elevator; they found him smashed to pieces. This event from long ago impressed itself upon his memory and slumbered there, in hiding for years, only to pop up again one day the way a corpse resurfaces when the stone on it is dislodged. Indeed, this had happened only a few months earlier, while he was standing by the elevator door in the editorial offices of a Berlin publishing house. He pressed the button and heard the humming of the old French elevator in its cage as it descended from somewhere on high. Suddenly it stopped right in front of him, abruptly, with a slight rattle, a polished black coffin, lined with purple silk imprinted with irises like the reverse side of a lustrous piece of *crêpe de Chine*; it also had a huge Venetian mirror, polished on the edges, with green glass like the surface of a crystal lake. This upright coffin, made to order for a first-class funeral and controlled by the invisible power of a *deus ex machina*, had descended from above, docked like Charon's ferry, and now sat awaiting the pale traveler standing there petrified and uncertain, the manuscript of his latest novel, *The Man Without a Country*, shoved under his arm (and through the grate he himself was observing the pale traveler in the mirror, standing there petrified and uncertain, with the manuscript of his most recent novel clenched under his arm). And the coffin was waiting to take him not into the "other world" but merely into the grim basement of the building, the crematorium and cemetery where glassy-eyed stray travelers rested in sarcophagi similar to this one.

3

When he reached his room, to which the porter had already delivered his luggage, the guest first spread his manuscripts out on the table and then began to jot down his impressions of the day. In the last few years the man without a country had been writing more and more frequently in hotel rooms at night, or by day in cafés, on tables of artificial marble.

4

He captured in haste a few observations, a few *Bilder*: a newspaper vendor slurping her soup from a plate, next to her nostril a wound the size of a coin, a raw open wound; a female midget attempting to climb up into a train; a waiter totting up a bill with his pencil between his little finger and index finger because the rest of his fingers were missing; and a pimply porter with a boil on his neck. And so on.

5

He despised duels as a symbol of *Junker* arrogance, in the same way that he scorned commonplace scandal and showdowns with fists or knife, but for all that he was no less obsessed with human cruelty, which he saw simply as a depiction of the cruelty of society. Physical deformity and every kind of abnormality fascinated him as the flip side of the "normal." Giants, dwarves, boxing champions, and circus freaks triggered in him a whole chain of metaphysical associations. Deaf from the noise of the fans, he watched their maniacal faces. Squeezed in amongst hysterical fans, he grasped, he sensed corporeally, the meaning of certain abstract concepts such as *community*, *leader*, and *idea*, as well as the connotation of that hoary adage about bread and circuses that sententiously presents us with the whole starting point of modern history.

6

Back in his homeland this poet had a monument, and streets, named after him; he had generations of admirers and his own mythos, as well as followers who praised him to the skies and stood in awe of his verse and lyrics as the pure emanation of the national spirit; and he also had sworn enemies who considered him a traitor to national ideals, a sell-out to the Germans and the Jews, the nobles and the moneyed classes, and these enemies denied that he had any originality, proclaiming him an ordinary imitator of the French Symbolists, a plagiarist of Verlaine and Baudelaire, and they wrote pamphlets about him full of accusations and every manner of slander.

7

His father, Aladár von Németh, began his "diplomatic career" quite modestly covering the shipping news for the *Pester Lloyd* newspaper, and his first posting was in Rijeka (Fiume). The journey to Fiume coincided with the honeymoon of this young diplomat who had just married a certain Zofia, née Dvořak. In that city of consuls and diplomats the future "man without a country" came into the world; he would retain for the whole of his life the memory of the sea and of a palm tree in front of his window, straining beneath the hammering of a gale, as an illustration of a Spartan proverb that was near and dear to his father's heart: the power of resistance is acquired through constant struggle against the elements.

8

His room was lined with carpets and the floor covered by sheep-skins; in summer the blinds were let down over the windows to shield him from the sun while in winter the sitting rooms were heated by a gargantuan tile stove that looked like a Secessionist cathedral. From the time he was five years old the nursery had been unheated, as a hygienic precaution and a part of his training in the Spartan mode; sometimes the nursemaids would lie down in the child's bed so that their wholesome commonplace warmth would fill the heavy feather duvet.

9

His great-grandfather on his mother's side (mutton chops, stove-pipe hat clutched in his left arm, his right resting at the elbow on a high shelf; on the shelf, in a vase, paper roses; at his feet a faience figure of a tremendous mastiff) was named Feldner. He didn't leave much of a paper trail around the house, with the exception of that photograph with the paper roses, and it was with a cer-tain feeling of guilt that they referred to him as "the late Feldner" (using his last name and always with the addition of "late"). That some ancient wrongdoing had come down from him, some type of original family sin—this was beyond certain. Hence the sparse documentation on him; hence the sole photograph in the album.

10

And this round face, with its big black moustache and hefty sideburns, that's the writer's father, Dr. Aladár von Németh, accompanied by Lajos von Hatvany ("who corresponded with T. Mann and Romain Rolland"). And here is the writer's mother (a cheerful face under a crown of blonde hair pinned up in plaits). And here we see the family in a boat, on a river. *Au verso*: "Belgrade, 1905." The high walls with the tower that one can almost make out in the background are the walls of the Kalemegdan fortress. —A clearing in the woods, with guests seated around a roughly hewn wooden table. The boy is sitting in his mother's lap; next to them is Dr. Aladár von Németh, with his hunting rifle, the stock of which he has leaned against the table like a *hajduk* would do; at the head of the table, a gentleman in a hunting hat; the women are also wearing hunting hats, and the men Hungarian tunics: "Dr. Aladár von Németh in the company of His Highness Ludwig III, King of Bavaria. Pressburg/Bratislava." —The boy on his bicycle. With one hand he's propping himself up against an ivy-clad wall: "Budapest, Rákóczianum, 1913." —The lad with a group of other schoolboys and professors; an arrow indicates Egon von Németh: "München. Wilhelmsgymnasium, 1914." And so forth.

9

11

With the help of a poet he discovered at an early age the mysterious, encrypted language of love. As an eighteen-year-old, in love with a fellow student, a German girl, he discovered that in this poet's works there was one poem for every phase of *amour* (for raptures, disappointment, dread, regret); and he commenced translating. And so he translated—"completely *à propos*"—fifty of the poems, and at the point when the love-cycle had quickened in the German language and was already in the printer's hands, love evolved for him, via the process of crystallization (to put it in Stendhal-ese), to that point at which passion begins to smolder and go out. All that remained of the whole youthful adventure and amorous delirium was this anthology of translated poems, like some dog-eared photo album. And that purplish echo around the issue of love in his novels, and that lyric tension in his sentences that was to be noted by critics, and not without a certain perplexity.

12

Every sensitive young nature, above all when it is flooded by education and music as in his case, tends to regard the powerful, turbulent fascinations of body and soul, that lyrical magma of youth, as precocious signs of talent. These natures are inclined to think that the issue is more often than not simply one of the secret quiverings of their susceptibilities, the imprecise teaming up of glandular secretions and sympathetic spasms, a symbiosis of their organism's tectonics and the music of the soul—those things that are the gift of youthfulness and intellectual precociousness and, similar to poetry in their tremblings, are easily mistaken for it. And once under the power of this magic—which grows over the years to be a dangerous habit, like tobacco and alcohol—a person will continue writing, with the skilled hand of a hack, writing sonnets and elegies, patriotic verse and occasional pieces; and it is now obviously just a matter of being a wound-up mechanism that lurched into motion in one's youth and now continues to turn, by the force of habit or inertia, at each and every brush of the breeze, like an empty windmill.

13

In that epoch, when the *Bildungsroman* was in full flower in European literature and writers were basing their work on the social origins of the protagonist (the "narrator," behind whom was concealed a slightly altered autobiography), in a kind of perpetual self-recrimination and escape from their own environment and in a belabored emphasis on their disloyalty, or, on the contrary, in that other version of *vanitas* that underscores the writer's ordinary origins, emancipating him from inherited sin and any fatalistic responsibility for the evils of this world, and vouchsafing him the divine right to label things evil with no contrition—it was in that period, then, that Egon von Németh consciously did away with the autobiographical elements in his work. He considered the question of his parents and origins to be a triviality and an accident of fate, even while intuiting with great foresight that in the theory of social origins there were signs of a new and dangerous theology of original sin, in the face of which the individual was helpless, marked for all time, with the stamp of sin on his brow as if put there by a red-hot brand.

14

"I am a typical mixture from the Habsburg Empire of blessed memory: simultaneously Hungarian, Croat, Slovak, German, Czech, and if I were to nose around in my genealogy and have my blood analyzed—which these days is a very popular kind of science in the world of nationalities—then I would find there, as in a stream-bed, traces of Tsintsar, Armenian, and, yes, maybe even Roma and Jewish blood. But this science of the spectral analysis of blood is one that I do not recognize. It is a science by the way of very dubious value; it's dangerous and inhumane, especially nowadays and in our region where this menacing theory of *Blut und Boden* engenders nothing but mistrust and hatred, and where this 'spectral analysis of blood and origins' is typically carried out in a sensationalistic and primitive manner—with a knife and revolver. I've been bilingual since birth, and I wrote in Hungarian and German until I was eighteen; that was when I translated that collection by the Hungarian poet and opted for the German language, because it's the nearest to my heart. I am, good sirs, a German writer; the world is my homeland."

(On the basis of this text, which forms part of an interview from 1934, one gets the feeling that "the late Feldner" in that family photo album might have had one of those dangerous "blood types" that the nationalists considered inheritable, like syphilis.)

15

First and foremost, this stand of his was the product of his organic resistance to banality. For the theory of origins, of *racial* ones on the one hand and social ones on the other, had taken on monstrous proportions in those years and become a commonplace amid all the misunderstandings and rapprochements: the great idea of community descended upon the *salons* and in the marketplaces. It gathered under its banner people wise and stupid, noble spirits and the dregs of society—people, therefore, who were linked neither by any personal affinity nor by any intellectual kinship but solely by this banal, hackneyed, and dangerous theory of race and social origins. That is why in the works of Egon von Németh, works that otherwise teem with representatives of all the social strata of Europe of that day—the nobility, the upper bourgeoisie, the middle class, intellectuals from every possible background, merchants and craftsmen, officials and functionaries, parasites and the *Lumpenproletariat*, workers, peasants, nationalists, soldiers, traditionalists, social democrats, revolutionaries—in these works the autobiographical elements are absent. The witness must be impartial; the grief and repentance of the one party must be as alien to him as the prejudiced thinking of the other.

16

The man without a country, the stateless one, the cosmopolitan—as he was labeled by the newspapers in his home country—traveled to Amsterdam in the middle of April, after making a long arc through Italy, Yugoslavia, and Hungary. Along the way he wanted to visit his old, infirm father in Pest and absorb the European climate so that he would have some fresh and reliable material for his new novel *Farewell to Europe*. From Pest, where he took leave of his father in the awareness that he would probably never see him again, he traveled on in this way to Amsterdam, where he negotiated with his publisher, a certain van der Lange, the same man who had published his first novel a year ago, in German.

17

Mr. van der Lange was one of those young publishers who—because of some sudden resolution—reorient their love of literature, and perhaps their talents as well, from the goal of uncertain literary fame to the much more secure business of publishing the types of books, and even the very books themselves, that they would have wanted to write (and could have written?). After inheriting his father's lending-library business, which was in addition part bookstore and part stationery store, Mr. van der Lange decided one day to print the books of his friends, having burned his own poems first, with a touch of regret. He was a lover of German literature; Heine was the first writer to poison him with poetic reveries and teach him the difference between the lyrical and the ironic, as well as the fragile relationship between them—a knack that is as hard to find among poets as it is among readers. In the 1930s, as German writers were becoming less and less able to find publishers in their fatherland, having been adjudged insufficiently transported by the national spirit or poisoned by the inheritance of their blood, Mr. van der Lange started publishing the books of German refugees, without being at all unfaithful to his preferences. The writers found in him not just a publisher of their works but also someone who gave them a friendly word and some encouragement. He was, in other words, one of those publishers whom success, money, and fame hadn't made arrogant and inaccessible, or who just went through the motions, seeing their writers as frauds and malingerers who, instead of doing real work, spent their time in pursuit of something entirely vague and pointless . . .

18

If it hadn't been for the papers (the stateless one read them early in the mornings, in the hotel restaurant) and their talk of armaments, of the dizzying increases in prices and unemployment, of diplomatic negotiations and anxious urgency, one could have believed, here in Amsterdam, that one still dwelled in the good old Europe of yore, and that the threat of war, Munich, the Reichstag fire—that they were all just nightmares and apparitions of a sick imagination. Mr. van der Lange, his publisher, a man with a jutting lower jaw and calm, gentle eyes (as if the bottom of his face were separated from the upper part by centuries of civilization), conversed with him over cognac and coffee, as if the two of them inhabited some island together. Mr. van der Lange was very well informed about the situation in Germany, and in their conversation he evinced—in spite of all the strict discipline that supposedly consigns men of good upbringing and high culture to lives of self-control and sangfroid—no little concern over the fate of German culture and the future of the continent. As for those matters strictly related to business, he again took care of these with the politeness of a man both realistic and sober, and he put together a contract with the stateless one about which neither of the signatories could be dissatisfied. But when the other man laid out the "German situation" for him on the basis of his own experience, that is to say as a witness, Mr. van der Lange grew morose, like a person hearing something horrifically unpleasant and difficult to refute about his very own mother.

19

After that nervous and depressed Europe where the people were gathering in the streets to catch the words of orators and demagogues on the balconies, and where armies were goose-stepping through the cities while masses howled in the stadiums, the man without a country suddenly found himself in Amsterdam on that bright April day, as if in another world altogether. The market women offered their goods with voices that were hoarse but merry and betrayed no trace of anxiety; the housewives continued flipping the big wriggling fish at the stands; the young men rode around quite civilly on their bicycles, pushing the pedals slowly and steadily, spokes gleaming in the sun. Next to the marketplace stood a huge barrel organ, painted orange, looking like an elegant coach and cranking out a medley of songs. Two girls in traditional folk outfits, with their white kerchiefs and yellow wooden slippers, held out to pedestrians tin cans bearing the symbol of the Red Cross. Boats moved calmly along on the canals; on one of them multicolored laundry hung on the ropes to dry, and someone on deck was playing the harmonica as if trying to imitate a canary . . . Through narrow uncurtained windows families could be seen around tables with steaming dishes of food: bright accents on idyllic scenes of family life, the way they would have appeared on the canvas of a Dutch master.

20

Here in Amsterdam, in a lonely little street a stone's throw from a canal, the man without a country looked up a fortune-teller one afternoon whose business was attracting attention with its over-the-top advertisements that no one could say were lacking in imagination: "What awaits you on the morrow? Only God and Satan know. And their pupil, Herr Gottlieb." And so forth.

21

He walked through the door, then pushed aside a heavy plush curtain and found himself plunged into reddish twilight emanating from a lamp with a red shade, lying on its side. After he had scanned the room, which seemed empty to him, he felt somewhat disappointed, as if he were experiencing *déjà vu*, as if he had already seen all of this somewhere. Above all it was professional curiosity that brought him to this "premium fortune-teller"; he wanted to have a complete mental inventory of the scene in case he should ever need to evoke it. But right away, right at the door, it dawned on him that he should allow this "soothsayer" to decide his fate, since he had already exhausted all other means: the advice of friends, priests . . .

22

Now he was seated in a second-class compartment of an express train, thinking about what Mr. Gottlieb, the "premium fortune-teller," had told him. The man's statement reverberated unceasingly in his ears, formulated in passable German: "Paris is your last chance . . . Yes, yes. The last . . ." Was he superstitious? No more and no less so than other people. If he had been told this earlier, two or three years ago, he would not have paid any attention to it.

23

Capturing on paper, in haste, and with no explicit, patent goal, these miscreant humans, this freak show, the man without a country was aware of the fact that literature was playing a secondary role here, even as he also tried hard to pretend to himself that his interest was a purely professional one, and involved human phenomena; it will probably, he thought to himself, turn out to be more of an exorcism of some type, part of that phobia that prevented him from entering an elevator, of that dread of the unknown that literature can only make use of as an exorcism. Because, ultimately, if he should need such a figure, it would rise up from his memory, even before he pored over his notebooks and jottings, and what he was doing now was thus serving as a kind of amulet to ward off the evil eye, or malevolent destiny. For he needed health, and he needed life, a healthy and normal life, since his unfinished work still lay before him—everything else was subordinated to that thought. Everything else.

24

The stateless one left his hotel at five. In front of the doors to the building he stopped for a moment and looked first up at the sky and then at his watch. "The marquise went out at precisely five o'clock," he noted to himself.

25

The blow came so fast, so unexpectedly, that our *apatride* couldn't have felt anything save the penetrating pain on the crown of his head; and all at once daybreak lit up all around him, as if a thunderclap had struck in the vicinity; lightning flashed in his mind, illuminating with its fearsome and powerful tongue of fire his whole life, and immediately thereafter darkness must have descended. His limbs separated from his body, as if an invisible force had ripped them from his torso. (We can, by means of analogy, have a presentiment of this horrific sensation of a higher power pulling the limbs from our body: once upon a time you were rocking on a chair and the chair suddenly flipped over, and you found yourself lying with the crown of your head on the concrete floor while for a moment your hands and your feet seemed to be separated from your body, ripped out of their joints, and you lay for several seconds without moving on the ground, incapable of screaming because robbed of your voice.) This rapid flash of light, like the flame of a torch before a hard gust of wind extinguishes it once and for all, this illumination prior to complete obscurity—this is as far as we are capable of following the experiences of the man without a country. Further than this (as Mme Yourcenar would say), we cannot go. No such experience has ever been vouchsafed us. And we will never be able to experience such things.

26

You, dear sirs, would like for me to show you the house in which I was born? But my mother gave birth in the hospital at Fiume, and that building has been destroyed. And you won't manage to put up a memorial plaque on my house, because it has probably been torn down, too. Alternately, you'd have to hang three or four plaques with my name on them: in various cities and various countries, but in this I could not be of assistance to you either, because I don't know in which house I grew up; I no longer recall where I lived during my childhood; I barely even know anymore what language I spoke. What I do remember are images: swaying palms and oleander somewhere by the sea, the Danube flowing along, dark green, next to pastureland, and a counting rhyme: *eeny, meeny, miny, moe* . . .

JURIJ GOLEC

I had just returned to Paris after the Easter holidays. I live in the 10th *arrondissement* and I do not suffer from homesickness. On sunny days, I am woken up by the birds, like in Voždovac. Through the open door on my balcony I hear the Serbs shouting and cursing at each other; in the early light of dawn, as they are letting their engines warm up, accordion notes come tumbling out of their tape players. For a moment I don't remember where I am.

I pulled the mail out of the box and started listening to my messages: Anne-Marie is letting me know that a new review of my book is out. (Just for the record: I had already read it.) Then some music, and giggling; I don't recognize any of the voices. B.P. from London informs me that he has no intention of conversing with phantoms, and I should throw this machine out with the trash. Then, giggling and music again. A certain Patricia Hamburger ("Yes, like the meat") reminds me, if I understand her correctly, that I flirted with her after a visit to an exhibition in some gallery, and that I kissed her hand. (It's possible.) After that, there were two or three hang-ups. And B.P. once more: if he gets this machine one more time . . . Then, probably grasping the fact that time is running out: "I have something important to tell you. As for this accursed little machine, throw it in the garbage. I want to speak with you, and it's quite a serious matter. But, damn it all, I cannot talk to a machine! I'd like to know what moron convinced you to buy this marvel. And why? It's not like you're some traveling salesman! I mean, really, what kind of all-important business dealings do you have? And those *women* of yours can just be patient for a bit . . . Incidentally, it would be better for you to write instead of . . . Did you really . . ." Yes, I know, that's all fine and good, but the thirty seconds are up and I still have no idea what important matter he wanted to share with me. Luba Jurgenson conveys her apology: the last sentence of her article was cut, and so the text sounds incomplete. And then a frail voice: "This is *Jurrri* Golec. My wife has died. Burial Thursday at four P.M. The Montparnasse cemetery." After that: Mme Ursula Randelis. O.V. from Piran. Kristos Arvanitidis, my friend from Thessaloniki. A certain Nadja Moust from Belgium; she would like to take a course in Serbo-Croatian; what are the requirements for registering. B.P. again, this time *in medias res*: "I just want to say that we've known each other for more than thirty years and we have still never had a *serious* talk. Farewell." After which the line went dead.

At least ten days had passed since Jurij Golec had left that message, so I immediately sent him a telegram of sympathy. Then I tried repeatedly, and at different times of the day, to reach him by telephone, but no one answered. I assumed he had left town. Later I found out from Ursula Randelis, a friend of his of many years, that he had moved into Noémie's apartment. (They had separated over twenty years ago; she lived by the Jardin du Luxembourg and he in the 14th *arrondissement*.) I called there a number of times, till at last I heard his faltering voice: "You've reached 325-26-80. *Jurrri* Golec and Mrs. Golec, also known as Noémie *Dastrrre*. Please leave your number."

One morning he rang me up: "*Jurrri* Golec here."

"Poor Noémie. Did you get my telegram?"

"Yes, thank you."

"I thought maybe you'd left town," I said. "It happened so suddenly."

"Never mind. I'm calling on an important matter."

"All right. Go on."

"You are a sensitive man, David. You'll understand." (Pause)

"I'm listening."

"You aren't like the French." (Suddenly he switched to Russian.) "*Ty poet*. That's not flattery. After all, I said as much in the foreword to your book. You're the only one who can help me. Money isn't an issue anymore. It doesn't matter what it costs. Noémie had plenty of money. I don't know if you're aware of that. She was working in ethnographic films and made a pretty penny. And then there were her African sculptures . . . Are you listening to me?"

"Of course I'm listening to you."

"She'd cut me out of the inheritance completely, but then right at the end she changed her will. In the hospital. She was of the opinion that I had atoned for all my sins in relation to her. She left the largest portion to a foundation in Israel that will bear her name."

"What kind of foundation?"

"For the study of the folklore of East European Jewry. Which is apparently in the process of dying out. But what she left to me is quite sufficient."

"So travel somewhere."

"I have to remain here. All the formalities pertaining to the inheritance, the official inventory . . ."

"At least move out of that apartment. It's not good for you."

"You have to help me."

I thought maybe he wanted to borrow money until the issue of the will was settled. Or maybe that he wanted me to help him move. He had a huge library with books in every imaginable language.

"I'm at your disposal."

At that point he burst out: "*Kupi mne pistolet.*" And as if he were afraid that I hadn't understood him, he repeated it in French: "Buy me a pistol. I can't go on like this."

"I'm coming to see you immediately. Are you calling from home?"

"Yes, from Noémie's apartment. You know where it is. Fourth floor, on the left."

He opened the door quickly, as if he had been standing there behind it the whole time. To me he seemed to be looking better than ever. There were no rings around his eyes, he was freshly shaven, and his lean face had a rosy complexion; he resembled a man who had just stepped out of the sauna. He was wearing a new, tailored suit made of lustrous fabric, a light-colored shirt, and a colorful silk tie. It was the first time I'd seen him dressed up like that. The finish on the wood of the furniture gleamed, and the windows were flung open, even though it was cool outside. Porcelain ashtrays gleamed on the table.

Right away it hit me that the African sculpture collection was missing. On the wall between two windows there was just one single female figurine with large breasts, and on the opposite wall two modern drawings were hanging in narrow black frames.

"I've got some good wine," Jurij Golec said, going into the kitchen; I heard him uncorking the bottle. Then he returned.

"I'll have one little drink with you. Otherwise, I don't drink."

"You must be taking tranquilizers. I did that myself when I was going through my divorce . . ."

"Alas," he said with a wave of his hand, "it doesn't help."

"A physician once confided in me that he took his sedatives with whisky."

"There's no point to that anymore," he stated. "I need a pistol, not pills."

"Excuse me, but you must admit that I also have a certain amount of experience in such things." (When Ana and I separated, I had a major crisis. Jurij Golec at that time comforted me with ambiguous words in the manner of a Talmudic sage: "Aside from getting married, there's only one other really stupid thing a person can do in his or her life: get divorced. But the greatest stupidity of all is to regret it.") "At night I put wax balls in my ears," I said. "And a black blindfold over my eyes. I took sleeping pills and drank. When I woke up, my bed seemed like a grave. I thought that I would never sit down at a typewriter again."

"You'll write much more," said Jurij Golec. "But in my case . . . You once said that you were on friendly terms with some Yugoslav gangsters in Montparnasse. You could procure a pistol for me with their help. She changed her will in the hospital. She considered my behavior of late . . ."

At that point the telephone rang. He started conversing with someone in German.

Why the hell had I told him about my encounters with those "Yugoslav gangsters" in Montparnasse? I wondered. Besides, he'd blown it out of proportion. They were for the most part friends from my high school years, and when I got together with them, they were hardly packing any weapons. Or, at any rate, I never saw any in their possession. They just told me stories. About a guy who'd just come out of Le Select, or about someone they claimed I knew ("the tall fellow with the moustache"), since we had sat at the same table the day before yesterday. This man had gotten stabbed to death the other day at the Place Pigalle. Yet another guy killed two Corsicans with his pistol a few days earlier. Or he had been shot dead himself—I don't remember anymore. A third got eight years: for smuggling weapons, and robbery, and pimping.

"One of my friends," Jurij Golec said when he returned to the table. "Hasn't left his house for ten years now. He tried to kill himself; the Metro took off both his legs above the knee. He lives on the eighth floor, but he lacks the courage to try it again. He drinks. Takes pills. And waits for death. Is that how you all want it to be for me?"

"I'll get a pistol for you," I said. "A year from now. On May 8, 1983. I have experience with things like this."

"In a year?" he said. "I won't be able to stand it for a month. Not for a week."

"In a year, in the event that you still have need of one."

27

"I thought you were different from the French. But you're just like all the rest. You don't understand me either. Why should I . . ."

"Because you survived the camps." (He had a number tattooed on his forearm.) "That's why. Someone who's lived through the camps . . ."

"Leave the camps out of this," said Jurij Golec. "Compared to this, the camp was a joy. Even Raoul, that unfortunate creature without legs, survived the camps."

We were already on the second bottle of cabernet sauvignon. It was then that I noted the wine was going to my head and that I was hungry; all I'd had for breakfast was coffee. I suggested we go out for a bite to eat. Or we could have a proper lunch together. I was sure he hadn't eaten anything.

"I'll take you someplace," he said. "Let's go eat, somewhere close by. I have to be back here by five at the latest. A couple of people are coming by. And the clerks from the court could show up at any time. Oh, for the day when all these formalities are complete!"

We walk through the *passage* and come out on the boulevard. The air is cool, although from time to time the sun breaks through the clouds. One can feel spring's incremental victory; the tables have been put out on the sidewalks; the women are sitting facing the sun, with their eyes closed and skirts pulled halfway up their thighs. A black man in shorts swishes past us on roller skates and then zips across the street. I watch as he goes out of sight into the Jardin du Luxembourg; on the gilded tips of the fence around the park the sun is leaving blood-red traces, like on some gaudy painting in the Louvre.

The restaurant has been recently renovated, and it still smells new. Lamps with red shades and gold tassels hang in the booths. Paper tablecloths cover the plastic tables. In the vases, artificial flowers, and next to them, in a metal rack, the holy trinity of French cuisine: salt-pepper-mustard.

In one of the alcoves, the restaurant owners are dining, a heavy blonde woman with painted fingernails and a corpulent red-faced man with a little moustache. With large knives they are slicing up bloody steaks. A bottle of red wine, unlabeled, stands on the table before them; the bottle is imprinting the paper tablecloth with red half-circles.

They greet us with handshakes.

"*Ça va?*"

"*Ça va*," says Jurij Golec.

"How's Madame?" asks the proprietress.

"She has died," says Jurij Golec.

The owner takes a swallow of wine.

"But it hasn't even been a week since Madame was here," he says.

"*Mon Dieu, mon Dieu.* Automobile accident?"

"Leukemia," says Jurij Golec. "We'd like something to eat."

"Have a seat there," the owner says, pointing to a table with his knife. "Or there. Gaston! Bring these gentlemen a menu. Yes, such is life. It just seems as if Madame had sat here only yesterday. Right there where you are sitting now. I'm afraid we're out of *menus d'hors.* It's three o'clock. I recommend you get the roast beef. Gaston!"

"Chicken for me," Jurij Golec says. "With fries. And a salad. She's been dead a month already."

"And what will your friend be having?"

"An omelet," I say. "And a carafe of red wine."

"None for me," Jurij Golec says. "I don't drink."

"Madame always took such good care of herself," says the proprietress. "Only ate healthy things. Eggs, fish, vegetables. And lots of carrots. Gaston, bring the man a fork."

"In the last few years," says Jurij Golec, leaning in my direction, "she ate only grass. Like a cow."

We went back to Noémie's apartment. On the way Jurij bought himself three cartons of Rothmans—ten days' supply, at least. He paid for my cigarettes, too.

"I also smoked Gauloises and Gitanes for years," he said. "Until I got French citizenship. I smoked that trash so I'd have the same taste in my mouth they have."

We had no sooner returned than he started in again:

"So then what you want is for me to hurl myself under a subway train, like miserable old Raoul. Don't interrupt me, please. Is that what you all want to become of me? And I, as you can see, am not in any condition to open up my own veins. I am horrified by the sight of blood, like the hero of your novel. Especially now. For a whole month I went to be with her in the hospital every day. I greeted the dawn at her bedside. With no tobacco or alcohol. I don't intend to go on and on to you about all that. About the blood, the vomit, the excrement, the pus. We were married for thirty-three years. We met in Poland, after we were released from the camps. She was on her way back from a Russian camp, I from a German one . . ."

"For the last twenty years we didn't live under the same roof. In that length of time I slept with a lot of women; I assume she took lovers as well. How many? I don't know. But there was nonetheless something that bound us together. Something elemental. Whatever it is that unites a man and a woman forever."

The telephone rang, and he chatted with someone else in German, quietly. Either German or Yiddish. Then he returned to his seat opposite me. "A month before she got sick, we went for a stroll on the Boulevard Saint-Michel. It was a clear day, like this one. At one point she stopped and took my hand. 'I would like to live a hundred years,' she said. 'With you.' And we kissed. On the lips."

Jurij Golec drank a swallow. "A splendid bottom line for an old Jewish couple," he concluded. "After thirty-three years of shared life."

"It would be a good idea for you to go away somewhere," I said. "What's the status of the will anyway?"

"There is the possibility that she left me nothing. I don't care. I only want the paperwork to be done with. But none of that is important now. I'm done for. I helped a few people. Slept with ten women. Maybe it was a hundred. I wrote this and that, might as well have been writing with my finger in water. I have no strength left, and no curiosity."

"I understand how you feel. I leaned out over the edge of this abyss recently too. People don't know what advice to give, and God, if you don't mind my saying, doesn't know His way around in such matters. At that time I started searching for books that would give me strength to keep on living. And I arrived at the tragic conclusion that all the books I had devoured over the decades were of no use to me in that decisive hour. I'll omit the holy books and the sages of old; I wasn't receptive to them, because I lacked the basic prerequisite of a belief in God, which you yourself have. I read the widest variety of authors and works: Gnostics and gnostic commentaries, *Surviving and Other Essays* by Bruno Bettelheim, Linden's *Autogenic Training, Les destins du plaisir* by a certain Aulagnier, Goethe's *Elective Affinities, La nuit, le jour* by Braunschweig, Herbert Rosenfeld's *Psychotic States*, the novels of Philip Roth, and even Hjalmar Bergman's *Marionettspel*, because I myself resemble a puppet whose strings are controlled by fate. The only thing I got from all this reading was the realization that books provide no answers to burning questions. That we are directed by our genes, the devil, or God, and that our will plays no role at critical moments, that we are simply knocked this way and that by our various passions. As when someone is swimming hard and the shore not only recedes but actually seems to gape wide, as the current—for you are swimming upstream—carries you in the opposite direction. But, fortunately, passions, like misfortunes, are transient; like all plants and animals too . . ."

I sensed that my words were coming across as hollow and bookish; it's not easy to respond to a person whose question is "Why should I be alive?" I was acting with the best of intentions: drawing on my own experiences, I wanted to make clear to him the beneficial effects of time, and to sketch the future out for him, his future: sitting somewhere on the Mediterranean coast, warming his bones in the spring sun, drinking cappuccino and patting the young waitresses on their rear ends.

"When all is said and done, you have to live, because this is the only life there is."

He waved his hand dismissively.

"Don't forget that I believe in God," he said. "And He'll forgive me."

This trying conversation was interrupted by the ringing of the doorbell. Jurij Golec introduced his guests to me by name and added: "My *protegées*."

He indicated to them that we were old friends and I was a writer.

"He wrote the foreword to my last book," I said, in order to conceal my embarrassment.

They were two pretty young women, with luxurious hair, pronounced cheekbones, and slightly tilted Tatar-like eyes.

"Oh, Jura, why didn't you tell us?" Nataša said.

"You see?" Dola continued. (She owed her name to Dolores Ibarruri.) "You at least have other people to live for! What vile things you've been saying! What do you mean, a pistol? *Boh s tobój!*" She then turned to me: "If Jurij wrote a foreword to your book, then it must be good."

I promised to send them copies of my books; the one with the foreword by Jurij Golec and, of course, the one about the camps. (They were the daughters of a Soviet general who had perished in the purges.)

"Cheers!" Nataša said after pouring everyone a drink.

"To your health," Jurij Golec responded absentmindedly.

"There are," Dola said, "so many beautiful things in this life. Friendship, for example. And, you see, we all need you. If you didn't exist, where would we two have taken refuge when we got to Paris? You can't even imagine what all Jura has done for us. His apartment is a veritable embassy for refugees from all over the East. For Russians, Poles, Ukrainians, Estonians. For everyone. How long have you known Jura?"

"For at least ten years," I said.

"We met at a reception, a long time ago," said Jurij Golec. "When his first book came out in French."

Note: This reception had been organized by Mme Ursula Randelis, a patron of South American writers. In addition to those writers, authors from other countries passed through the side door, so to speak. The cocktail party took place on the occasion of a book launch, for a Portuguese, a Spaniard, and me; the books came out in a series devoted primarily to Latin American writers. I knew no one and didn't dare to eat anything, because I didn't know how to break open and eat crabs and shellfish; so I sat there the entire evening with a canapé and drank. At three o'clock in the morning a young woman suggested driving me to her place, and I threw up in her bathroom, lying there on the floor, half-dead. Fortunately, people forget things that are earmarked for oblivion. Over the course of the years the memory of that hapless reception had evaporated, and an insuperable obscurity would have descended upon it if Jurij Golec hadn't brought it up again two or three months ago. He asked me whether Marie La Coste had written anything about my new book. I told him I didn't know who that was. "Chivalry is an attractive personality trait to have, my dear friend, but you know you slept with her. This is an open secret. At that reception chez Ursula Randelis, you kissed her hand under her husband's nose. And toward daybreak the two of you ducked out."

"I thought she was one of Mme Randelis's domestics," I said. "I was actually amazed myself at how large her bathroom was. With pink tiles and a bidet."

To steer the conversation to other topics, I stated:

"I think that you two should persuade him not to go on living in this apartment."

"You see, Jura? Everybody agrees that it's not a good idea for you to live in her apartment," said Nataša. "We've told him that a hundred times."

"Just until the formalities are complete," Jurij Golec said.

"So, in the meantime let's get to work," said Dolores-Dola, and the two women stood up simultaneously. "The sculptures are gone. That's good. Never mind the ashtrays, Jura; I'll empty them. What do we do with this?"

We were standing in the next room, where Noémie's library was housed. The books were arranged over an entire wall, stretching all the way up to the ceiling.

"These are valuable books," Jurij Golec said, taking down a volume of *The Jewish Encyclopedia.*

The women ran their eyes over the shelves and each of them pulled out a book at random.

"These are new books," Dola said. "Tomorrow we'll take whatever interests you over to the apartment by car. As for the rest— the used bookstore!"

Jurij Golec was standing in the middle of the room with a volume of the *Encyclopedia* still in his hand, not knowing what to do with it.

"Some of them are autographed," he remarked.

"It's not like she's got one signed by Victor Hugo," Nataša said. She was crouched down on the floor, running her fingers over the worn carpet in Noémie's room as though picking a fabric swatch. "This is a Persian," she said and pointed to the carpet in front of the dressing table, upon which, as in a poem by Baudelaire, little glass perfume bottles were lined up.

"Tomorrow we'll come with the car for all that," she said. "Vladimir Edmundovich, M. Brauman, and the two of us. Do you see, Jura? Everything will be taken care of."

"And what's in there?" Dola asked, indicating the cabinets in the foyer.

"Her stuff," Jurij Golec said after laying the encyclopedia down on the radiator and opening one of the cabinet doors. "Toward the end she was buying fur coats. She complained about the cold. She even wore them around the apartment. She claimed that she was feeling the effects of the extreme cold that got into her bones forty years ago in Siberia. *Pustjaki,*" he added with a dismissive wave. "She was thinking of moving to Africa permanently."

"There are some good furs here," Dola noted. "They should also be sold. This one alone cost at least 20,000 francs."

Jurij Golec added: "120,000. She only wore it once. Last year. For Yom Kippur."

"For what?"

"For a holiday."

"There are at least thirty pairs of shoes here," Dola said.

"In Russia," said Nataša (who had emigrated only recently and was still making use of anti-communist propaganda), "this could all be sold for hard currency in a *Beryozka.*"

"*Boh s tobój!*" cried Dolores-Dola. "What do you mean, a *Beryozka*? We should donate this to the Red Cross."

"Maybe some of it, via the *Croix Rouge*, will make it to Afghanistan," Jurij Golec said, casting a glance at the clock.

Then the doorbell rang.

"Doctor Wildgans," he said, as if to himself.

Dr. Wildgans was a tall man of approximately thirty, with curly, luxuriant hair, already decorated with patches of white. There was something wild about him, something "Bedouin-like"—and not simply on account of the unusual color of his eyes, greenish-yellow, and the large shawl that he had tossed over his shoulders. Two weeks ago he had returned from Afghanistan. He had crossed the border with two other doctors and, dressed as a combatant, trekked through trackless mountains. He had observed ambushes from his hiding place; and through binoculars he had watched armored vehicles be abandoned by their crews; he carried out a number of amputations in a tent, under the most primitive conditions, about a hundred kilometers outside of Kabul.

"You have helped so many people," Jurij Golec blurted out. "It's just me you won't help."

"Take two at bedtime," Dr. Wildgans said and set a little bottle of pills on the table. "These are more effective."

After the two women had left, it felt as if a heavy layer of fog had once more settled over the room. The muted hum of the city was audible; music from one of the neighbors' flats seeped through the walls. Somebody was stubbornly practicing chromatic scales on the saxophone; now and again the notes merged with the howling of ambulance sirens.

"You can talk freely in his presence," Jurij Golec said, turning to Dr. Wildgans.

"You can't demand it of me. I am a physician."

"That's precisely why. You are a physician, and I require an effective treatment. Cyanide. Or a pistol."

"These pills will help you."

"All right," Jurij Golec said. "So you two want me to hurl myself from a fifth-floor window. To end up a cripple. Like miserable Raoul. You know Raoul. Or slice open my jugular. 'My loved ones and friends shied away, seeing my wounds, and my fellow men are remote.'"

Suddenly he arose and picked up the ashtray in order to empty it. He left the bathroom door open as if he feared we might conspire against him. I heard him urinate and then flush the toilet.

"I don't have it in me to open my veins or hang myself," he said, as he returned with the now gleaming ashtray. "I can't imagine myself with my face all swollen and blue, and my tongue stretched out . . . I've seen enough scenes like that in my life already. Let me assure you: a hanged man is not a pretty sight, not in the least. Even the fact that I could have one final ejaculation doesn't much thrill me. If it's even true that one ejaculates from the gallows. Can I take these with alcohol?"

He was holding the little bottle in his hand.

"I wouldn't recommend it," said Dr. Wildgans.

The next day I called him again.

"You've reached 325-26-80, Madame Golec, or Noémie Das-tre. Be so kind as to leave a message and your telephone number. Good-bye, and thank you."

It was Noémie's voice. It was coming either from heaven or from hell; it doesn't matter which.

On Friday I went to Lille to teach my classes. I had about ten students; my classes were on "one of the languages that make up the great family of Slavic languages, along with Russian and Polish . . ." I tried to make use of Mme Yourcenar's sensational acceptance to the *Académie française* in order to introduce the students to the Serbian folk poetry that Mme Yourcenar held in high esteem, as her book *Oriental Tales* demonstrated. The students had not read Yourcenar. So I tried using love poems. In sonnet form. But they didn't know what a sonnet was. I tried it in alexandrines, like Racine. (No doubt just some bourgeois scam.) So I switched to palatalization and the death of *yat*. Apparently that held some interest for them. They wrote it all down in their notebooks. Therefore I myself had to bone up during the train ride on palatalization and the death of *yat*.

Saturday I called up Ursula Randelis.

"Noémie's voice is on the answering machine," I said. "I felt like I was talking with the Hereafter."

"He shocked me with that message, too," she said.

"He demanded that I get him a pistol."

"He asked me for that too. Don't worry. You weren't the only one. He always had a sense of drama. I know him well. I've known him for thirty years or so. My God, how time flies. Noémie's death rattled him. I can understand that. It came so unexpectedly. The doctors themselves weren't completely certain. She always just had this temperature, and you see? In less than a month. I don't know how much you know, but they'd lived apart for twenty years. May she rest in peace. But she had a bad temper. And no understanding for him. Why should he only sleep with one woman his entire life? He's not a rabbi, after all! She couldn't stand me, either. It was no secret: I had been his lover. Back when I left the convent. Twenty years ago. Twenty-five. Since then we've been friends. The best of friends. I don't understand what in hell this voice on the answering machine means. Sorry, but someone's at the door."

After a brief pause:

"My son. He's learning Spanish. Blood is thicker than water. I won't hold his hand through it. Just so you don't do drugs, I tell him. Jurij Golec is like a child. He's incapable of paying his telephone bill. Lord only knows how many times they've cut his phone off. Then Ursula swoops in to set things right. It's the same with the power, and with the rent. With everything. And do you think Noémie ever lifted a finger? Never. He needs a mother. Or a sister. 'How are you doing, Jurij?' I ask him. 'Everything's fine,' he'll reply. 'Just fine.' 'But I can tell that something's not right,' I say. 'The inability of the human being to adapt to existence,' he says. 'That's all it is.' And now he has this inheritance on his shoulders. It is a torment for him. How is that going? I have no idea. Apparently the will hasn't even been read yet. So that's why he hasn't budged from the apartment. I told him he should give the key to that little Japanese woman. There's a Japanese woman living next door. A student. I wonder if he's slept with her. Of course Noémie couldn't stand her. At any rate he should get out of that apartment as soon as possible. And stop being so dramatic. What's with the pistol? Between you and me, it is possible that she left him nothing. Not so much as a cent. She was certainly capable of doing that to him. He'll have told you about it. So, fine, it's her money. She earned it herself, and it's hers to dispose of as she wishes. Jewish folklore or African sculpture—it makes no difference to me. Just let things get settled already. At any event, people should give him some peace and quiet now . . . You were right to tell him that: a year from now everything will be all right. As if I hadn't been through crises myself. Show me a normal human being who hasn't experienced a crisis. When Angel Asturias abandoned me, don't you think I had a crisis then? Oh, I had one, and how! I drank, I took pills, the works. Excuse me, the doorbell again. It's a madhouse here. I-am-com-ing! Call me again in the next day or two. I'm snowed under with work. Translating Cortázar right now. Don't know if it'll amount to anything. Whenever you want. One minute! I'm coming! You can also call late at night. Till one. Or two. Or even later. I'm coming! *Mierda!*"

On Sunday I was invited to Madame d'Orsetti's. Since her divorce from a Parisian gallery owner, she lived by herself in her large apartment close to the Parc Monceau, and she threw dinner parties for a group of intimate friends. She was wrapped up in astrology, all kinds of collecting, and fashion, which, according to Baudelaire, is included among the arts. She devoured horror novels and put away large quantities of sleeping pills and white wine.

She was a good friend of Queneau and Perec, and she knew de Chirico, René Char, and Dado. As her guest, one drank tequila, whisky, vodka, and white wine originating in her own vineyards. She spoke of herself in the third person: "D'Orsetti went jogging at six o'clock in the morning in the Parc Monceau; d'Orsetti has a fever of thirty-eight degrees Celsius; d'Orsetti is going to London tomorrow; d'Orsetti is inviting Armani to dinner."

I was surprised to see that she had designated a place at the head of the table for me, since the widow of Prince S., who had been a literary critic and translator, was also invited to this dinner, along with the famous fashion designer Armani. Considering this an instance of her deliberate lack of conventionality ("d'Orsetti hates conventions"), I sat down at the place to which they ushered me; I didn't want to stand out as someone who paid too much attention to formalities.

The conversation was about people I didn't know, or themes that didn't interest me: fashion, feminism, pederasty, conceptualism, comic strips. But the main topic of the evening was an opera that I hadn't seen, and more particularly a young vocalist who had debuted in this production. Madame d'Orsetti thought her appearance plebeian, her voice common, and her interviews stupid; on the other hand Armani, who managed to win over a majority of those present, asserted that a new star had been born and would soon be shining on the operatic firmament of Europe: a new Maria Callas.

Even those people who had a completely negative view of Madame d'Orsetti, claiming she was a lesbian and an alcoholic, admitted, however, that she had great culinary talents and gastronomical imagination. As appetizers on this particular evening she served us caviar, tuna with black butter, and carrots in cream, and for the main course, "carp-in-the-sand" and lamb with rhubarb and walnuts; following that there were cheese and ice cream (pistachio and pineapple) with a sauce of crème de cassis. Along with this they brought us a 1967 white, "d'Orsetti,"—on its yellow label stood the maxim "*In vino veritas*"—as well as a Bordeaux for those who didn't wish to align themselves with the tastes of the lady of the house.

After the dinner, Mme d'Orsetti, enveloped in a purple shawl, sat on the floor and rocked, barely perceptibly, to the rhythm of music from the gramophone (Rameau, Brahms, Vivaldi). At some point she put her glass down on the rug and nodded at me to follow her. When we reached the bedroom, she indicated that I was to take a seat on a bed with a violet baldachin; she passed me a glass and filled it to the rim. While pouring the vodka, she had said:

"Your friend Jurij Golec has committed suicide. I wanted you to dine in peace first. Now I shall leave you alone. If you feel the need to talk with someone, d'Orsetti is at your disposal."

The burial was set for Tuesday, at four P.M., but the ceremony started almost an hour late. Apparently people here are used to it, because when I showed up, right at the appointed time, there was nobody at the cemetery yet. I thought that Jurij Golec's friends would be gathered at the graveside or in front of the chapel; but then Luba Jurgenson, an acquaintance of mine, showed up and we waited together in front of the cemetery gate. Toward five

43

o'clock a crowd began to gather. We wondered if they had really come for the funeral of Jurij Golec. They must have been asking themselves the same thing when they saw us standing there, shivering in the cold wind. Finally Luba, an émigré writer and one of Jurij Golec's protégées, recognized a mutual acquaintance; she went over to a woman in black and embraced her. "Jurij's sister," she remarked to me. "She's just now come from America." Dolores-Dola and Nataša showed up in the company of a young man wearing a cowboy hat and striped pants; it was yet another Russian émigré, a painter, according to Luba. Finally there were about thirty of us: Emil Cioran, Adolf Rudnicki, Ana Novak, a literary scholar and former camp inmate; representatives of the Gallimard publishing house, the cultural attaché of the Israeli embassy, a delegate from the Jewish community, as well as various friends and admirers.

Mme Ursula Randelis kept her word and, contrary to my expectations, did not come to the burial. That same morning she had told me:

"I don't like dead people; I only like living people. The last time I was at a funeral, it was for my mother, twenty years ago. Then I made an exception, for Jurij's sake, and went to Noémie's, barely a month ago now. That will suffice for the rest of my life. Oh, now who's going to call me a 'crippled old mare'? Who will say to me, 'You horsey old goy, they cut off my phone again!' And who will tease me with 'Hey, you lazy biddy, let's go wet our whistle'? The next time I go to a cemetery . . . Come to my house after the burial, all of you. I don't know the Jewish customs; they aren't in my domain. I'll prepare something to eat. And we'll drink a glass of vodka to his soul. But I will not go to any more funerals. Not until the day it's my own."

The rabbi was a man of about fifty, trim, clean-shaven, in a black caftan, and had none of the bearded biblical prophet about him; more than anything he resembled one of those French judges in a robe whom one encounters in the cafés around the Palais de Justice. With arms extended, his palms turned up, he beckoned us to come over with one finger: "Come closer and gather about him, as you did in life. Closer, closer still, ladies and gentlemen."

The coffin was up on a podium set on one of the cemetery paths, under a large sycamore. In the widest part of the lid a small rectangular window had been put in, as if it were some kind of special Noah's Ark that would transfer the body of the traveler to the shore of eternity. Gleaming metal letters were affixed to the lid: "Jurij Golec, 1923–1982," like a perfectly condensed biography for an entry in *The Jewish Encyclopedia*.

When the rabbi had started to speak, I noticed Dr. Wildgans; his powerful figure had materialized behind a gravestone. That probably accounts for the impression I had that he didn't come in from the drive but from the field of graves.

Ever since Mme d'Orsetti had informed me that Jurij Golec had taken his own life, my suspicions had fallen on Dr. Wildgans. And this belated appearance of his, somehow furtive, fed these doubts. I tried to read his thoughts: was he feeling remorse? Or was he proud, perhaps, like a man who's done his duty by his neighbor? Ultimately, being both friend and doctor, it was he, I thought, who could best judge the validity of his decision; to slip an ampule of cyanide to a man who viewed death as salvation, or to procure a pistol for him. My misgivings were further corroborated by the fact that Dr. Wildgans was the last person with whom Jurij Golec was seen alive; on the evening I've described, I had left him alone with the doctor. Perhaps Jurij Golec had finally succeeded in changing Dr. Wildgans's mind by the force of his arguments.

On account of the noise from the street and the indifference of people in big cities, there seemed to be no one who had heard the shot. The Japanese woman next door hadn't been at home. So no one knew exactly when he'd done himself in. The police were conducting an investigation but weren't interested in filling in the details for the curious.

Should I have helped him? I wondered. I actually could have gotten him a pistol, through my Yugo-thugs, with no great risk to myself. My conscience hadn't let me rest, in the meantime. I'd kept imagining him lying there on the sidewalk, bleeding, his skull shattered; or how the blood would stream out of his veins; or how he would hang there in the cabinet among Noémie's furs, skin gone blue, his tongue jutting out and his eyes popping from their cavities. Now I felt like a person who had failed to hasten to the side of someone in mortal danger; like a coward who had left his friend in the lurch.

This sentiment was compounded with feelings of guilt of another sort: since everyone knew that I was one of the last to have seen him alive, I had the impression that they suspected me. Mme Ursula Randelis had repeated the following menacing formulation to me two or three times over the phone: "If I catch the bastard who provided him with that pistol . . ." And it seemed that the threat was aimed at me.

Dr. Wildgans liberated me from this nightmare. As if he intuited my suspicions about him, he came over and gave my hand a very prolonged shake. He told me about Jurij Golec's end: he had purchased a hunting rifle and some big-game ammunition; he'd pointed the barrel at his heart. He'd left the receipt for the weapon on the table, too, as written up by the saleswoman, as if to avoid any misunderstandings and to prove that we were all naïve bumblers and that he was not as inept in practical matters as we thought. On the reverse of the receipt he scribbled in an agitated hand his Kafkaesque last will and testament: "Burn my papers."

In the text that the rabbi read aloud, I recognized a brief passage that had been printed twenty years ago on the cover of Jurij Golec's one novel: "Born in Ukraine in the years immediately following the civil war, Jurij Golec, once a prisoner at Auschwitz, has lived in Paris since 1946. After pursuing Asian studies in Poland, Germany, and at the Sorbonne, he worked as a correspondent for various foreign newspapers. His one novel—he was, as one says, a man of one book—was written in French." Then the rabbi listed all the volumes of poetry and essays, and he particularly emphasized the major role that Jurij Golec played in the awarding of the Nobel Prize to Elias Canetti. "He helped his neighbors; he prayed facing toward Jerusalem; in his own way, he believed in God."

When the rabbi began reading the Psalms, alternating between Hebrew and French, five or six men put on the yarmulkes they pulled from their pockets. Dr. Wildgans placed a twice-folded handkerchief on his head.

The rabbi read, holding his Bible on the casket as if it were a pulpit, supporting himself with his fists on the lid: "My soul drew near even unto death, my life was near to the hell beneath. They compassed me on every side, and there was no man to help me: I looked for the succor of men, but there was none."

And he continued in Hebrew: "Adonai, Adonai."

"O Lord, rebuke me not in thy wrath: neither chasten me in thy hot displeasure. For thine arrows stick fast in me, and thy hand presseth me sore . . . I am feeble and sore broken: I have roared by reason of the disquietness of my heart. Lord, all my desire is before thee; and my groaning is not hid from thee . . . My lovers and my friends stand aloof from my sore; and my kinsmen stand afar off . . . Forsake me not, O Lord: O my God, be not far from me. Make haste to help me, O Lord my salvation."

This was a distant echo of King David's voice, pressing toward us from the obscurity of time and history; it was the testimony of an inspired and afflicted poet, written some three thousand years ago, that still reaches our hearts like a knife and like balsam.

"I cry out to you, Lord, saying, 'You are my confidence, my portion in the realm of the living. Hear my lament, for I am much tormented; save me from those who persecute me, for they are mightier than I. Lead my soul from the dungeon, that I might praise your name. The righteous will gather around me, if you are favorably disposed to me.'"

Next to the grave, on the edge of the marble slab, I caught sight of a dead rat; it lay on its stomach, as if resting for a moment; its tail, stiff and straight, lay draped on the ground like a standard in defeat. What led it here? What worked its death? I wondered. Was

God's providence perhaps at work here? Jurij Golec, a connoisseur of the Talmud and the Upanishads, would certainly have found an explanation for this phenomenon, and would not have seen any provocation in it. Then I remembered: "A few late rats, like bulky army tanks, are making their way home to their boathouses." So it's a rat from that simile of his, I thought; one that has come straight from his novel to the Montparnasse cemetery. Because nothing is stable apart from the grand illusion of creation; no energy is ever lost there; every written word is like Genesis.

I stood by the grave and observed. Hugging the stone and seemingly contorted, ants stretched out their wispy antennae in the direction of the huge swollen body, not daring to attack it. And the dead rat, the living rat from the novel, lay there motionless, still unmarked by any visible signs of decay, like a heavy armored vehicle; its treads had been blown apart by an anti-tank mine and its crew had abandoned it.

"I sink into the deep mire, where there is no bottom; I fall beneath the water into the depths and the spate will cover me. May my prayer rise up before you; incline your ear to my wailing; for my soul is full of woe, and my life approaches the inferno . . . You have placed me in the bottom of the deepest pit, into the darkness and the abyss."

Using ropes, the gravediggers lowered the casket into the hole that had been dug next to the drive. The letters on Noémie's headstone were already starting to dull; the marble plaque resembled an iceberg that had survived the winter; on the bare wires of the wreaths scraps of crepe paper hung, washed colorless by the rain.

As we moved past the opening, we threw handfuls of earth onto the coffin, the same way one used to throw stones onto dead bodies in the desert so their skeletons wouldn't be scattered by wild animals. One of the gravediggers was carrying a little wooden chest with earth from Jerusalem; the earth was light in color and loose and was mixed with desert sand. The wreaths were all leaning on Noémie's grave. One of them read "For Jurij Golec—may God forgive you." I understood, even though the name of the benefactor wasn't listed: "I only like living people; I don't like dead people." I knew who was capable of leaving so harsh a message, which was also a sign of love.

I waited around until the undertakers had put the marble slab in place. It was identical to the one on Noémie's grave. Then I helped them arrange the wreaths, and divide them fairly. After so many years the two of them were resting under the same roof again, like a pair of lovers from the old days; not in the same grave, but still next to each other. After thirty-three years of shared life.

"An excellent bottom line for an old Jewish couple," I said to myself.

Postscript

The name Jurij Golec is not invented; it's merely one of the names that my unfortunate friend Piotr Rawicz assigned the narrator in his one novel, *Blood from the Sky*. Thus his presence in this story has remained halfway between reality and the world of Platonic concepts.

The price of the fur coat seemed exaggerated to me at first, and I was prepared to lower it arbitrarily by knocking off a zero. Fortunately, just as I was finishing this story, I found an ad in a newspaper (from November 19, 1982) for a large store specializing in furs; a Russian sable at that time cost 106,000 francs after the 15% discount (original price: 125,000). Thus I learned, six months after taking a look into the closet of the woman known here as Noémie, that her most expensive fur coat was a *zibeline* (Russian sable), that it was worth precisely the amount given in the story, and that J.G. had not exaggerated. Aside from these utilitarian facts, e.g., the price of a fur, I discovered an entire array of exotic fauna and subsequently went over Noémie's wardrobe in my mind, that wardrobe where so many furs of inscrutable origins shimmered: mink, silver fox, arctic fox, lynx, Canadian wolf, astrakhan, beaver, nutria, marmot, muskrat, coyote; and these have now, *voilà*, found their way into the story through the back door, after the fact, unleashing new sensations, opening new worlds: *métiers*, market forces, money, adventure, hunting, weapons, knives, traps, blood, animal anatomy, zoology, far-off exotic regions, nocturnal animal noises, Lafontaine's fables; great are the temptations of a tale. In contrast to a novel, however, one may not, in a tale, open the doors of cabinets with impunity.

THE LUTE AND THE SCARS

Although I had sworn never to set foot in the place again, one evening, after a two-year absence from Belgrade, I dropped by the Writers' Club. I'd had plenty of opportunities to convince myself that associating with authors was difficult, fraught with misunderstandings, jealousy, and insults. And I was also aware of the fact that this kind of intellectual struggle, *éscrime littéraire*, bitter and sterile, is part and parcel of the literary trade, just like writing reviews and checking page proofs. On this point I remembered a piece of advice that Chekhov once gave a young writer, challenging him to leave the provinces and mingle with the literary crowd in the big city; once he'd gotten to know them, he would draw less idealistic conclusions about writers.

It was early autumn and warm out, and people were still seated in the garden. An undertone of voices was audible, along with clinking silverware and tittering women. Upon entering I took a look at the guests and discovered with astonishment that in the two years of my absence nothing had changed; they were all sitting in their old places and appeared to be drinking the same bottles of wine that they had ordered on the last evening I was here. It was just that the women were a touch more voluptuous, and the men, graying at the temples, had let their bellies go. The rings under everyone's eyes were even darker, and their voices had become more gravelly still from drink and tobacco. With my back turned to the garden there was now only one table in my field of vision, the one under the gnarled tree, closest to the entrance. Two middle-aged men I did not know were sitting at the table, along with a round-faced woman with bleached-blonde hair and small, lively eyes. The woman kept giving me a little smile.

"Don't you recognize me?"

I shook my head.

"Anjutka," she said. "We met once at Nikola's house."

Now I remembered.

"Don't burn your bridges behind you," I repeated under my breath. "How are you?"

"I got married," she said. "This is my husband."

She looked like a shaggy old dog. She was constantly brushing the hair out of her eyes; she tossed her head back coquettishly, causing the flabby skin on her cheeks to shake. She was one of those women who don't understand how to grow old, who add to the misfortune of aging a grotesque mask of youthfulness. It was easy for me to calculate how old she was. Back when I slept with her, she had been thirty-nine; I had been twenty-three then; and since that time about fifteen years had passed. "I could have been your mother," she told me. "Almost." In those days I lived in the vicinity of the Dunav railway station. She demanded that I retain the formal mode of address. "*This* doesn't give you the right to speak casually to me," she said; then she would go back to rolling her eyes and imitating the throes of passion. In the morning I walked her to the streetcar stop and told her we wouldn't be seeing each other again. She answered me with a proverb: "Don't burn your bridges behind you." She was right. A week later I looked her up again. "I've been thinking of you, Anjutka." In the morning I awoke on her maternal bosom.

In those days she worked as a guide for Russian tourists and traded on the black market. She succeeded in selling me Bulgarian rose water (tiny ampoules in a wooden container that resembled a salt cellar), a portrait of Pushkin in bronze bas-relief on a pedestal of Caspian marble, and Blok's selected works in three volumes (Moscow, 1958). I knew that these were gifts she had received from Russian tourists . . .

She leaned across the table toward the other men and related something to them in a low voice while shaking her head. I observed the fatal workings of time on her face.

I had the waiter take her a bottle of wine, and after I'd eaten my soup I started to leave. It was going on three in the morning. When I tried to get past her, she grabbed my sleeve.

"You weren't at Nikola's funeral," she said. "You must have been abroad again."

"Yes, I was."

"There were only four of us there to walk the coffin to his graveside. He died in his sleep. They found him a week later. I don't believe he suffered. Here's my card. Call me sometime."

I was listening to her voice as if from a distance. I remember shaking hands with both men, one of whom was her husband.

Then I went down Francuska Street toward the Republic Square and then on towards the Hotel Moskva. The shop windows in the *passage* of the Zvezda cinema were still lit up; dust had gotten into the fabric on the buttons for sale, changing their colors; dead flies covered the glass bottoms of the display cases as if they were dried-out aquariums. The pre-dawn sky was purple with the far-off harbingers of sunrise. When I was in the *passage*, I heard the jangling of an alarm clock; in a window facing the courtyard a light went on.

The courtyard entrance was barricaded with rotten planks; there were rows of rusty trashcans in front of it. A cat leapt out from between them and raced right past me. I peered through the decayed boards; inside it was dark and reeked of urine. I thought I could hear the squeaking of rats. I walked back out to the road. At the corner I started down Balkanska Street. Through a metal fence I saw a warehouse in the first light of day. The wall separating it from the house in which I'd once lived had been torn down, and the windows of the house had been removed and the roof demolished. In the shed stood a truck loaded with bricks and crushed rock next to enormous rolls of cable. I suddenly became aware of birds twittering, and I looked in their direction. A large sumac tree leaned over the courtyard, its foliage still green and swaying, as though anticipating the imminent sunrise and not simply buffeted by the breeze. I remembered: people can cut sumac back, but a new shoot will always poke up somewhere else. It can penetrate stone or concrete.

During my final years as a student I had found a room in the center of the city—the dream of all students, especially those from the provinces. That gave you not only a certain amount of social prestige but also the advantage of staying late in the cafés without the fear of missing the last bus and then having to wait till early the next morning—chilled to the bone in the wintertime (an experience familiar to all of us). The apartment was located in a *passage* and had entrances from two different streets. If you went through the *passage*—with its display windows for leather-goods stores, for stores that would mend nylon stockings, sell fountain pens and buttons, do alterations—you came out in a courtyard of little paving stones. At the far end, on the left, was a recessed doorway that led down to the lower level of the building, facing Balkanska Street, via a set of steps made of worn brick. The building was old and had just two floors. There were Turkish balconies and walls from which the plaster was crumbling, warped window frames, and a shaky wooden door. My landlords were elderly Russians, emigrants who'd come during the 1920s, a married couple without children. They rented out my room for a sum that covered a part of the electric and water bills; one could say they let it out more or less *gratis*. I had been sent their way by a certain Anjutka, a tour guide. I had met her on Skadarlija Street, thanks to some Russian writers whom she was supposed to hand over to me so I could take them to an official dinner in the Writers' Club.

I slept on an iron army cot, while the other bed, on the wall opposite, was occupied by Nikola, one of my landlords. Marija Nikolajevna, his wife, slept in the smaller second room, which also served as the kitchen.

Because I was often out of the house—by day in the library, in the evenings at the club—I was satisfied with my new lodgings;

they worked fine as a free place to lay my head, and one that was in the city center to boot; I had access to a bathroom with hot water, and my landlords didn't hold it against me when I came home late.

Marija Nikolajevna was a sickly, somewhat sarcastic woman with a puffy face that was disfigured on one side by traces of burns. Her hands showed the damage too; scalded, contracted skin was drawn taut over muscles and tendons; her fingers resembled claws. Marija Nikolajevna seldom set foot in the "men's quarters." She would knock on the door, stick her head into the room, and let fly some incontrovertible observation: "I know you don't own anything except this guitar. You don't have to lie." Or: "Somebody threw up last night in the bathroom. I hope it wasn't Nikola. Next time it needs to be cleaned up better. Good night." Or: "Yesterday, the bathroom was completely filled with smoke. You weren't even home. This means Nikola has started smoking. It's all due to your bad influence." (In a very stern voice:) "He's also taken to drinking with you. He *never* used to drink before. With you around he's become a bohemian too."

Nikolaj Aleksinski was an old man with an upright bearing, short gray hair, and smiling blue eyes. He was as deaf as a doorknob, but that didn't dampen his spirit or his good cheer one bit. He got up early, showered with cold water all year long (while you listened to him exclaiming "hu-hu-hu" and "ha-ha-ha" from the bathroom), and fasted one day every week, on Friday, for health reasons; on that day he drank only spring water that he had brought home from somewhere in a big demijohn. But this all had nothing to do with that nearly obscene resistance to death so typical of the elderly; this was more like a military kind of mental discipline paired with simple hedonism. I learned how to carry on a conversation with him by means of a kind of sign language. Our alphabet consisted of schematically reproduced letters from the old Cyrillic alphabet once used in Russian, and it contained symbolic abbreviations as well: touching one's hair with a finger indicated the first letter of a word or the word itself: *v* as in *volosy*, hair; touching a tooth yielded *z* for *zub*, tooth; pressing your palms together gave you *d* as in *druzhba*, friendship. It sufficed to get across the first letters of words to him; once the word was underway, he completed it out loud while looking you straight in the eyes.

I show him: thumb and index-finger in the shape of a Cyrillic *s*, then close the circle by pressing my fingertips together (*o*), and touch my hair (*v*) . . .

"Soviet," he says.

I sign: *l, i, t* . . .

And he finishes the word by saying "literature": "Soviet literature is still in its infancy," he maintains. "Like new grass. One must be patient while it grows."

I tell him (using my fingers): "Something is forever trampling on this grass."

"Yet no one can stop the grass from growing," he says. "Do you see that sumac tree out there in the courtyard? It grew up out of the concrete. Take a look at it."

I say: "But people—"

He guessed my thoughts: "People can cut it back as much as they like; somewhere a new shoot will always come forth. Force its way through stone, or through concrete."

I ask him, "Did you know Prince Ževahov?"

He stares at me in amazement. "Where did you pick up that name?"

I reply: "I read his book about Sergei Nilus."

Nikolaj waves his hand.

"Ževahov lived in Novi Sad until recently. The Russian emigrants have their headquarters in Sremska Mitrovica. Ževahov was an unfortunate case. With age his mind dimmed considerably. He saw ghosts. Don't you have anything better to do that to concern yourself with the likes of that mad Prince Ževahov?"

"I'm collecting eyewitness accounts," I say. "In connection with Nilus, he wrote about *The Protocols of the Elders of Zion*. What did this Ževahov look like?"

"In his youth he was attractive, tall. The last time I saw him was back before the war. He was still wearing his old-fashioned *pince-nez* and an Order of St. Nicholas on his shabby old dress coat."

I give Nikolaj the manuscript of my first book. (It would end up being published three or four years later.)

"It's as if you belonged to the circle of the Serapion Brothers," he says. "There are hints here that you share the same artistic program. Your reality is a poetic one."

I say something to the effect that poetic reality is still reality.

"Reality is like grass and earth," he says. "Reality is the grass that grows and it's the feet that mangle it."

I tell him that this is also a poetic image. A metaphor.

"An image, perhaps," he says. "Let's have another round. This is homemade kirsch. Some friends brought it to me. A writer," he went on, "is supposed to observe life in its totality. The writer has to point out the great theme, dying—so that humans might be less proud, less selfish, less evil—and, on the other hand, he or she must imbue life with some kind of meaning. Art is the balance between those two contradictory concepts. And a person's duty, especially for a writer—and now you'll say I'm talking like an old man—involves leaving behind in this world not work (everything is work) but rather some goodness, some knowledge. Every written word is a piece of creation." He paused. "Listen to that: the birds are singing already. Let's turn in. Marija Nikolajevna will be angry if we go on like this till morning. She's had a difficult life. Very difficult."

I never had the nerve to ask him what kind of conflagration left its terrible tracks on her body. Just as I also never came to learn anything about his own life. From my "acquaintance," the woman who had called my attention to this apartment and recommended me to the couple, I knew only that Marija Nikolajevna "had suffered burns while escaping from Russia" and that Nikolaj Aleksinski had come to Belgrade by way of Constantinople and was a specialist in forestry (a profession that I later assigned to the fictitious protagonist of one of my stories, in memory of Nikolaj Aleksinski, who already struck me as fictive, even back then). Although I spent many nights in conversation with this lively, good-hearted old man, I never heard so much as a single sentence from him spoken in confidence. I figured that my own shared confidences would make him my debtor, that he would one day grow communicative. But despite my confessions he never revealed anything about his earlier life.

I say to him: "What . . . should . . . I . . . do? I . . . am . . . in . . . love . . . with . . . two . . . women."

At once his face assumes an expression of sincere concern. His eyes, twinkling with encouragement, betray the fact that my romantic woes have touched his heart.

"Love is a frightfully tricky thing. Don't hurt either one of them. And don't rush into anything. For your sake, and theirs."

I say: "You've met one of them . . . I introduced her to you a month ago."

"Clytemnaestra," he comments. "A real Clytemnaestra. She's capable of doing serious harm. Harm to herself or to you. Love is a terrible thing. What can I tell you? One can't learn anything from the romantic experiences of other people. Every encounter between a man and a woman starts off as if it were the first such meeting on earth. As if there haven't already been billions of such encounters since the time of Adam and Eve. You see, experience in love is nontransferable. This is a great misfortune. And a great piece of luck. God set things up this way. Just one more, and then I'll put the bottle away. Marija Nikolajevna would be upset. Be careful. Don't hurt anyone. Our souls carry the wounds of love longer than anything. And take care that literature doesn't come to be a substitute for love for you. Literature is dangerous that way too. Life can't be replaced by anything."

Sometimes I asked him to play on his lute for me. When he was in a good mood, he'd say, "Tune it for me. I know you know how to do it."

I would tune the lute and he'd start to play. He knew a few *lieder* and some Gypsy romances by heart. His ears had gone deaf but a few melodies still tingled in them, like distant memories; and he would make these remarkable sounds as he played, as though humming to himself.

"I think it sounds good today," he'd say.

I would nod in agreement.

"That's because it's cloudy outside," he stated. "The lute has been drying out. But weather like this suits it. Is it in tune?"

Leaning over the instrument as if he was listening for something, he strummed a few chords. Then he looked me in the eyes.

"A-minor," I responded.

"It's cloudy outside: the humidity does it good."

I continued visiting him for years afterward, long after I had moved out. When my spirits were low, or when I needed advice, I would look him up. I knew he was reading all my writing in the journals, along with the reviews of my books.

"Talent is a curse," he said to me. "Pushkin suffered on account of his talent. People envy nothing so much as a divine gift. Prodigies are rare, while mediocrity is legion. It's an unending struggle. And don't you go bury yourself in books. Travel. Listen to people. And listen to your own inner voice. Now, Marija Nikolajevna is expecting to see you too. Don't get upset if she scolds you from time to time. She's sick. And unhappy."

Marija Nikolajevna, wrapped in a threadbare woolen shawl, was sitting by the window. The window gave onto a gloomy courtyard surrounded by battered walls.

"I read in the newspaper," she said, "that the theater company you work with is going to Russia. Are you going along?"

"Yes," I answered. "We're going on a fifteen-day tour."

"That's what the paper said. Could you do us a favor?"

"I'd be happy to."

"I've written down two addresses for you here. The first one is my sister's: Valerija Mihajlovna Ščukina. The second is for Marija, like me, Marija Jermolajevna Siskova. That's her best friend. Once she was my best friend, too. The last letter I received from either of them was in January of '56. So, nine years ago. There's a chance that they're both still alive, or at least that one of them is. I assume that there would've been somebody to notify me if they had died. But just in case, take this—another name. Karajeva. Natalija Viktorovna. She's the youngest of all of them. Let me write down her address for you, too. She could tell you what became of them, in the event you can't find those first two. Would it be too hard for you to do this for us?"

On the second day after our arrival in Moscow, I was able to bribe the stern-looking caretaker on our floor. In front of the entrance to the hotel an invalid in a shabby army coat was standing propped up on crutches; he held out his greasy cap to the passersby. I gave him a bit of change. He tendered his thanks as though reciting a passage from Dostoyevsky.

I had barely turned the corner when I came upon the taxi stand that I'd discovered the day before, during our official tour of the city. The taxi took me to a large apartment building with a grim entrance and long, cold corridors.

I approached a couple of girls who were playing by the door. They looked at me, flabbergasted, and then scattered without a word. Finally a woman showed up and I read off the name and address to her.

"I don't know," she said.

"Who else can I ask?"

"I don't know. There are a lot of tenants here."

I didn't intend to give up. Once inside the building I figured out how things were numbered and what the abbreviations in the addresses meant; they represented the doorways, floors, building wings, and then individual apartments. At last, when I'd figured out the note, I knocked on a door. After a long pause, I heard a woman's voice: "Who is it?"

"I'm looking for Valerija Mihajlovna Ščukina."

"She doesn't live here."

The voice came from just behind the planks of the door; I knew that the woman was observing me through the peephole.

"Maybe you know where I could find her?"

"You're a foreigner?"

"Yes. A foreigner."

I heard the woman unlocking the door. She stuck out her head.

"Let me have a look at it."

I gave her the address. "Do you know any of these three people?" I asked.

She shook her head.

"We've only been living here for three years. Ask over there, down at the end of the hall. Last door on the right. Ivanovna. Varja Ivanovna Strahovska. She might know."

Then she handed me the piece of paper back; I heard her locking the door.

I knocked slowly, cautiously. No one responded. At some point it dawned on me that no one was behind the door, and I pushed down on the handle. The room measured about five meters square. A lightbulb without any kind of shade hung down from the ceiling. In the corner was a massive stove, like the ones in factory canteens. I understood then that this was the communal kitchen for the whole wing of the building. Feeling like I'd stumbled onto a secret hiding place, I exited quickly and closed the door behind me. But my inspection had apparently not gone unnoticed.

"What are you doing here? Who are you?"

The woman was enveloped by a large knit shawl; she wore her hair done up in a big bun. On her feet were stiff army boots.

"Excuse me," I said, handing her the paper with the addresses as if it were an official form. "They told me that Varja Ivanovna lived here. Strahovska."

"You're a relative of hers?"

"You could say that."

"A foreigner?"

"A foreigner."

"Varja Ivanovna is very ill. Her heart. Wait here."

She knocked on the door right across from the community kitchen; she disappeared for a minute and then reappeared.

"She says she has no relatives abroad. Or anywhere else."

"I'm a friend of Marija Nikolajevna Aleksinka. Tell her that. She'll know."

The woman went back into the room without knocking again. This time she was gone longer. At last she emerged.

"Go in for just a bit. I take care of this building. You should have called ahead. Go on in."

The room resembled a cell. Bare walls. A bed against the wall, and next to it a stool. A glass of water and a little bottle of prescription medication on the stool. A pale gaunt woman lay with her head on a thin pillow, covered up to her chin with a singed army blanket.

"I am Varja Ivanovna Strahovska. I heard who you are. You were asking about Natalija Viktorovna Karajeva. She died two years ago, in this same bed. She was a friend of Marija Jermolajevna, who died four years ago. No, it was five. I knew Marija Nikolajevna Aleksinka too. And her children. They died in a fire. I'm glad to hear that she's still alive. Her sister, Valerija Mihajlovna Ščukina, was the first one to die, about eight years ago. Well, now I'm dying in turn. I've told you everything I know, so please leave me in peace. I don't feel up to remembering anymore, or talking either. I'm preparing to die. Meetings in this world mean nothing to me now."

"Forgive me, but I'd like to be able to tell Marija Nikolajevna a bit more about her sister. And all the others."

"What is there to tell you? There are lives that it turns out weren't worth living. We lived as if we were dead. Farewell."

She closed her eyes, a sign that she was ending our conversation. At that point the door opened. "So, you found her alive after all," said the woman with the bun in her hair. "Now go, before I call the cops."

For months following my return from the tour, I put off visiting my old landlord and landlady. But one day, walking past the Zvezda cinema, I looked them up. First I walked into Nikolaj Aleksinski's room. He was reading Berdyaev. I shared my impressions from the tour and told him about the visit to the Novodevichy Cemetery and the Lenin Mausoleum. He served me kirsch.

Then Marija Nikolajevna appeared in the doorway.

"Pardon me," she said. "I don't want to disturb your carousing. I just wanted to check in with our traveler. Is he still unlucky at love?"

"We're talking about Moscow," I said. "And Leningrad."

"Ahhh," came the reply. "But then what can you see in two weeks? Nothing."

"I saw Dostoyevsky's grave," I countered. "And Blok's."

"You see?" Marija Nikolajevna said, appealing to the old man with her hands. "I told you he would forget to look for my sister. He did nothing in Russia but drink vodka with the actresses. He's a bohemian."

"I couldn't get away from the group. That's not easy to do in Russia." (Then I translated it into our sign language.)

"I knew it," she said, leaving the room.

"No matter," Nikolaj Aleksinski commented. "It's better for you to have gone drinking with the actresses than to have roamed about Moscow. It really is better this way. For *her* not to find out."

I realized it was obvious to him that I had carried out my assignment.

"Let's have another glass," he said. "Then I have to put the bottle away. Marija Nikolajevna is very sick."

Postscript

In this piece, under the influence of Truman Capote, I attempted to approximate, in my own way, the genre of the "nonfictional story," in which the role of imagination is reduced to a minimum and the facts are everything. In my story "Jurij Golec" I didn't succeed in carrying out this intention: when a story's characters, even ones of secondary importance, are specific people who are still alive, the writer is sometimes compelled to make costly adjustments and concessions with regard to *amour-propre*, something that is as understandable as it is human.

THE POET

At dawn a notice had appeared near the power plant, on a wooden post.

It was autumn, the end of a wet and dreary October. The wind plucked the foliage from the poplars, in gusts. Leaves blew up and all around, like leaflets tossed from an airplane, and then descended to the ground.

The sign was hung on the pole with the rusty thumbtacks that someone had prized with his or her fingers from the death notice of one Slavoljub (Bate) Rapajić (1872–1945), a disabled pensioner, hanging below. The culprit did however show some respect for the dead: the new sheet of paper, no bigger than that on which the necrology had been printed, was only attached by means of two of the available thumbtacks; this meant that the death notice too was still hanging on the pole, fastened at both ends and still able to withstand the wind.

The paper-stock was yellow, of wartime quality, and in the course of one night or one morning it had browned considerably, to the color of withered leaves; as if, in this environment of autumnal

69

fading, surrounded and grazed by the poplar leaves, the paper had obeyed the laws of mimicry. Its tiny Cyrillic letters—very blue and quite pale—had already begun to wash out in the rain; in all honesty, however, the typewriter ribbon that had been used to type up this text hadn't been in the best condition to begin with.

The main thing to be cleared up was who, on that fall morning of October 25, 1945, had been the first to notice the sign—"in the immediate vicinity of the power plant, attached to a wooden pole with 2 (two) thumbtacks obviously removed from a notice of death on said pole."

This unimpressive scrap of yellowed paper ("half a sheet of typewriter paper of No. 3 quality, folded and cut with a sharp object"), the same size as a death notice, might indeed have gone unnoticed by the citizenry. "This is where the weather factor comes into play: it rained the entire morning, with only a few breaks, and a cold north wind was blowing. The majority of passersby were carrying umbrellas and for that reason did their passing by hunched over, fending off the gusts of wind and the showers of rain. Furthermore. it is necessary to take into consideration the fact that this portion of the street leading to the power plant is somewhat remote and is little used by pedestrians. Apart from some of the residents of the new public housing projects (two buildings) and some employees of the power plant, hardly anyone passes this way. The residents make use of the new road, the one that runs along the back of the plant, along the edge of a field. (The old street has been torn up by bombs and tank treads.)" And so on.

But that it would have gone *entirely* unnoticed, even if it was raining cats and dogs out, right up to eleven o'clock—now that just can't be.

As such, Budišić took his investigation in the following direction: Who had walked by on that morning, the 28th of October, 1945? When? And why?

First of all, let's have a look at the residents of this New Town housing complex. (This housing project, incidentally, is not new; it was built before the war and has remained unfinished.)

In Building Two (No. 1 has been destroyed) lives a certain Donka, Donka Bojačić, née Žunić, a retiree. Her son fell—on our side—during the war. She didn't manage to get away—for "medical reasons."

Her subtenant Đorđina Prokeš studies at the teachers' college, twenty-two years old, from a Partisan family: left her house about 7:30 on the day in question, toting a man's umbrella; didn't notice anything. ("You can trust her, seeing that she's a Party member . . . " etc.)

Building Three: the Ivanovićes: father Stevan, sons Dane and Blažo. Daughters Darinka-Dara and Milena, mother Roksanda-Rosa. (Took the Chetniks' side. Active for some time in the enemy's employ. Under investigation. Dane carries an automatic pistol around in the city. They've been interrogated. I caught up with them when they were dead drunk. Alibi verified: the night before and right up till ten A.M. they had been celebrating the mother's birthday: Rosa, whom they call *Madame*. Impudent behavior. "Arrogant." Do not own a typewriter.)

In the electric power plant there are four workers, all members of the Party. Supported our National Liberation Struggle. Alibis verified. Don't own typewriters.

A certain Pajkić had left for home about seven A.M., after the night shift. Near the plant he ran into Steva Ličina. Ličina lives at the other end of town (in the Zekić complex).

Who else could be a suspect?

The pupils of the elementary school named after "Pinki the War Hero."

And thus the circle closed. In the center of this circle, as in a mousetrap, was Mr. Ličina, Steva Ličina, pensioner.

What moved the retiree Steva Ličina to write verses directed against the Party and government is hard to say. Their exact content isn't even known, since Budišić, on the same morning that Ličina was arrested, burned them in the "mother of all stoves." Accordingly, we know only this much (or perhaps a bit more): the poem was typed on a (Cyrillic) typewriter and spoke in a deceitful and slanderous manner of the National Liberation Struggle, the Party, and Tito. Ličina was a quiet, diminutive, unprepossessing man. He wore a French cap (beret), and was always properly dressed and shaven even though he lived alone, a widower. Before the war he'd worked as an official of the provincial government. He was a clerk ("a pen-pusher") under Bodnarov (who fled to America) in the Ministry of Schools and Education.

As we said, the poem by Mr. Ličina was destined to have a short life, and no one knows (and we don't believe anyone will ever learn) its exact content, either, especially not the offending lines. It's true that Budišić had read the poem, yet he couldn't recall a single line of it. I mean, nothing at all. That means that only the most important thing stuck with him: that the poem offended his (Budišić's) sensibilities and "spoke disparagingly of the Party, the National Liberation Struggle, and Tito."

How many lines were in the poem?

Budišić asserted: More'n thirty!

Mr. Ličina: Fourteen. It was a sonnet. Renaissance style. Two quatrains and two tercets.

Budišić: Don't lecture. Just talk.

Mr. Ličina: I've told you everything. Two quatrains and two tercets. Two times four makes eight, plus two times three, which is six. Together that makes fourteen. A sonnet.

Budišić: Nope, there were at least thirty! Or more!

Mr. Ličina: I tell you it was a sonnet. Dučić and Rakić wrote sonnets too.

Budišić: They were traitors.

Mr. Ličina: Perhaps Dučić was, I'll grant you that . . . but Rakić was a patriot.

Budišić: How come you wrote it? Who told you to do it? Who were you in cahoots with?

Mr. Ličina: I sincerely regret it.

Budišić: Too late, too late . . . You should have thought of that earlier.

So they led him away into investigative detention. These were the days when the new regime had not yet consolidated its power, and the Chetniks, "bushfighters," and other renegades were still hiding out in remote districts. Sometimes they would come down into the cities and—in the coffee houses, under napkins—leave behind messages such as: "Mile Kožurica ate here, Chetnik rebel. Long live King Petar!"

Budišić, accordingly, had more serious matters to deal with than the case of Mr. Ličina. One day he was summoned to Kosovo, where the "bushfighters" were wandering around wreaking havoc, so Mr. Ličina remained in detention for two or three months. He was a model prisoner. He mingled little with the other inmates, and he barely ever spoke. Sometimes he recited, half to himself, this or that verse. Dučić and Rakić for the most part. ("Thus they say to us, children of this century . . ." and so on. Or: "Tonight, my lady, at the prince's ball . . .")

In January the interrogations began. He was now being questioned by a certain Projević.

"So, Ličina. You wrote a poem against Tito and the National Liberation Struggle. Do you know what we were doing with the likes of you less than six months ago? You know exactly what. You know. Remember that I'm not Budišić. Remember that. There'll be no dilly-dallying with me. Go on, spill it. Who put you up to this? Who helped you write it? At whose behest? Who paid you? Answer each in turn."

Mr. Ličina: I have already answered everything forthrightly and freely.

Projević: Leave your feelings of sincerity out of this, you miscreant. What do your feelings have to do with it?

Mr. Ličina: Believe me, sir, I don't remember anything else.

Projević: Should I help your mem'ry along a bit?

Mr. Ličina: I admit that the verses were inappropriate. Morally I bear full responsibility.

Projević: And you say you don't recall a single line?

Mr. Ličina: No. I give you my word of honor. I wrote the verses at four in the morning. Composed them at the typewriter.

Projević: Go on. Keep talking. We have a lot more important things to do than this.

Mr. Ličina: Then I put on my coat and picked up my umbrella. Forgive me, but what's become of my dog?

Projević: Well, look at him go. He's back on the dog kick again. I told you: we're feeding him every day, three times a day, with sausages and Dalmatian prosciutto. We're giving him milk, as if he weren't a dog but a lamb. Now just go on.

Mr. Ličina: I thank you for that . . . I'm relieved to hear it.

Projević: You took your coat and umbrella and went out into the street. Did you show the poem to anyone?

Mr. Ličina: Not to anyone.

Projević: Whom did you run into along the way?

Mr. Ličina: I cannot recall. Nobody.

Projević: This is really rich. Just great. Doesn't remember the poem, doesn't remember the people. But don't play naïve with me. You're no fool if you know how to write poems against the Partisans and against the people. We'll fix you right up. Oh, yes we will. Don't you worry about that. Here's a pencil for you, and paper, and now produce some poetry, my friend. To your heart's content.

Mr. Ličina: Thank you, sir.

Projević: Don't thank me, you worthless piece of . . . You act like this is a gift. Now get lost.

Mr. Ličina: Thank you, sir.

Projević: I don't want to set eyes on you till this poem is finished.

Mr. Ličina: I understand, sir.

Projević: How much time will you need . . . Let's say three months?

Mr. Ličina: Three days would be quite enough.

Projević: Nonsense! Three days? No way. Write it and revise it for three months. Till it looks like it was written by Zogović. Get it? Like Zogović? Or Mayakovsky . . . . Now get a move on!

So Mr. Ličina passed three months in solitary confinement, working on his schoolboy composition. He wrote and rewrote exactly as Projević had told him to do. First he composed a sonnet with an *abba* rhyme scheme. Then he changed it (keeping the words) into *abab*, while leaving the tercets the same. Ultimately he modified the tercets and discarded both of the final rhymes ("Front" / "Piemont"), because they sounded old-fashioned to him. And then . . . his paper ran out. That meant he had tried all the variants. There was nothing for him to do but wait. After exactly seventy-four days, he was led before Projević.

"Let's see it, poet," said Projević.

Mr. Ličina handed the paper to him across the table.

Projević: Sit down, sit down. Why are you looking at me like a deer in headlights? . . . Here, in the nice chair, you bastard. *Riiiii-ight*. Let's have a look-see.

Mr. Ličina sat on the very edge of the armchair, holding his beret in his hand. (It was the only piece of civilian clothing he had on.) He smelled the aroma of coffee and closed his eyes, as if he were drowsy. (He was probably thinking of his dog. Who could tell, with senile old grandpas like this one?)

Projević yanked him out of his reverie.

"From the bottom of my heart—this is good. Congratulations!"

Mr. Ličina: I tried hard.

Projević: That's plenty obvious. Bravo. So you see, you can do it when you want to.

Mr. Ličina: As far as the rhyme goes, the poem is beyond reproach.

Projević: Don't exaggerate.

Mr. Ličina: I gave my all.

Projević: Your all, you say. All you had? . . . Well, ol' Ličina, you don't know what it means to give your all . . . Don't you think, you shit, that a better rhyme might still be out there? Eh? Well, look for it. We have time, Comrade Ličina; we have tons of time. The future lies before us, the future in its entirety! So get rolling and don't let me see your face again until the poem sounds like something Mayakovsky wrote. Do you understand? Children should recite your poem at school festivals, and soldiers should sing it from the ranks. Here's some more paper for you . . . Think that's enough? Now beat it . . . Take him away . . . Good luck, poet.

Projević sipped at his cup of now cold coffee and started going through his stack of papers again.

Then he looked up.

Projević: Are you still here?

Mr. Ličina: I just wanted to ask, sir . . .

Projević (slapping his palm against his forehead): Aha, I had almost forgotten . . . Now we're feeding him with American canned goods from the Ministry's warehouse. He's gotten twice as wide as he is long. I give you my word.

Then he plunged back into his files.

In the course of the next three months (the year was '47), Mr. Ličina went through more paper than a rat. So much so that Projević sent this message via the guard: "The director is asking whether you are eating the paper, like a rat?" Meanwhile, a performance was held in the prison in which some actors from the city recited

Mayakovsky and other poets. Mr. Ličina was aglow with the fever of creativity. He didn't like the Mayakovsky. It was a long way from Dučić-Rakić. Quite a long way. And with no rhythm. Sloppy rhymes. His sonnet was better, much better. Objectively speaking. Without even considering his biography and background. If a Partisan or some younger poet had signed his name to it, this poem would have made him famous. But now . . .

He placed a whole stack of papers on the desk in front of Projević.

"O Ličina the Pathetic—what's all this stuff?" Projević asked.

"They are poems, sir."

"Ah, so they are. Poems. And you, Ličina, you think we're playing school here. You think I have nothing more important to do than read your poems. Or to select them *myself*. Get cracking! I don't want to see you for another three months. Not until (he glanced at the calendar on his desk), not until September. Have we understood each other?"

Mr. Ličina was as silent and meek as a wet poodle. Disappointed, no doubt.

"I'm asking you nicely: do we have an understanding?"

"That's fine, sir."

"Well now . . . Good. You can go. Oh yeah, I almost forgot. Your bitch had puppies. Six of them about yea big (shows him with his hands), like bear cubs."

Mr. Ličina said nothing, his head hung low.

Projević: What's up? You aren't satisfied with that?

Mr. Ličina: But it was a male!

Projević: A male, you say. I thought it was a bitch . . . Well then, I've gotten it mixed up. So somebody else's bitch had puppies.

In September Projević showed the poem to some important people in the Party. A number of them said: outstanding. The rest shrugged their shoulders: for no real reason.

Projević (drinking his *lozovača*): Cheers, comrades.

Everyone: Cheers!

Projević: So, Comrade Ćićko, this means you don't like it.

Ćićko: But I didn't say anything.

This conversation was taking place in the office of the prison warden. It was a kind of inspection. Between colleagues.

Projević: A traitor wrote this. An enemy of the people.

Ćićko: The one Budišić arrested?

Projević: Yes, that one.

A pause ensued. Then they began talking about Budišić.

Projević: I'll show you all the variants. Seven, eight of them. Each one better than the last. I just think it's a shame that Budišić didn't keep that first one.

Ćićko: It's a pity.

Projević: I'll show them all to you.

Ćićko: Sit down and stop acting like a child.

Projević took a seat.

They had another glass. And then another.

Projević: How about I bring him to you? So you can see how he recites.

Ćićko: Bring him.

He was delivered to them.

Mr. Ličina was squeezing his cap in his hand. They offered him a brandy. He thanked them.

Projević: Go on, recite the final version. So Comrade Ćićko can hear you.

Ćićko: Go on, go on. Don't be stuck up . . . If you were able to write like that . . . See, I give you my word: if the poem is good— we'll release you. But make it pretty . . .

Projević: Like last time.

Mr. Ličina started reciting his sonnet in the manner of the actors at the recent performance for prisoners. Or so his recitation seemed to him. He raised his arms to the heavens (the ceiling), laid his hand over his heart, and took a bow when he finished. He all but curtsied.

Projević looked at Comrade Ćićko. Then he said:

"You're free."

And they released him.

Mr. Ličina signed the certificate of release and the confirmation that he had retrieved his personal effects: his suit, watch, fountain pen, hat, shirt, underwear, vest, tie, raincoat, handkerchief, riding breeches, socks, shoes (low-heeled, yellow, size 37), ring of keys.

The guard accompanied him to the prison gate.

Mr. Ličina walked toward the city on foot. It was raining and the wind tore the foliage from the poplars. Leaves whirled up and around, like leaflets tossed from a plane.

A bit before nine he reached his home. He called out his dog's name: Lunja! Lunja!

The dog didn't respond.

When Mr. Ličina opened the door to the apartment, the reek of stagnant air greeted him. He ran his finger through the dust on his desk. The top of it gaped bare; his typewriter had been confiscated.

Then, without taking off his coat, he started up the water heater in the bathroom. While the water was warming up, he started to dust in the other room.

He checked the water with his finger, and then he got undressed and stepped into the water that was warm, almost hot.

He took a long bath, huffing and puffing, and almost broke out in song. (But people would have heard him. Auntie Mara had seen him going into the building.) Then he rubbed himself dry using a clean towel that he took off a stack of ironed linens in the cabinet.

He held his shaving soap in his left hand, and with his right he spread the foam over his face, making very slow circles, reminiscent of a tango. Then he squirted a great deal of cologne into his palm and rubbed it in, first on his face and then on his chest, where an old man's white hairs protruded. Lastly he puffed his cheeks up like a gargoyle and patted them with lotion-covered hands. His dry skin soaked up the moisturizer like the desiccated earth sucks in water.

Then he slowly put on his clothes, all of them clean and fresh. (Though everything smelled slightly of mothballs and uncirculated air.) Underwear, undershirt, shirt. Fresh pants (he took only the suspenders from the old pair), a fresh waistcoat and suit jacket. Clean socks, knee-high. He wiped the dust from his shoes with an old handkerchief.

Then he beheld his appearance once more in the mirror.

He tossed the damp towel from the clothesline into the bathroom, unhooked one end of the line and then jerked the other free of the wall together with its nail. He spread some newspaper (*Politika*) over a chair; it had been in his bathroom since before his arrest. Then he tied the cord to the hook from which the light fixture hung, and placed the noose around his neck. And he shoved the chair away with his foot.

THE DEBT

After a few "terrifying days," things unexpectedly calmed down in the morning. The doctor knew that this calm was only illusory and provisional; he knew that inside this sick human organism certain changes were taking place, changes whose nature was entirely unknown to science and that depended on God as much as on the complicated mechanisms of the organs and psyche. The sick man lay on his back, buoyed lightly by pillows; a monitor tracked the steady beating of his heart. His body was hooked up by tubes to complicated instruments that, for one, flashed how his organs were functioning onto a screen; in addition they ensured that he was artificially fed, and they eased the work of his exhausted veins, bowels, and respiratory system. In the peace of the bright white room only the quiet hum of this machine was audible, along with the occasional tinkling of glass pipes when the sick man moved his limbs even a little. For a while the patient looked up at the bottle suspended above his head, the bottle from which dripped the fluid transmitting life-giving sustenance, by means of a clear tube, into his body.

His staring eyes had dimmed a bit, and he was cross-eyed too, in the manner of people who usually wear glasses but have taken them off.

All was still, to look at him from a remove.

Slowly the drops fell from the bottle; they welled up and then slid suddenly into the tube. And just as one drop was flowing down along the clear piece of tubing toward his body, the next drop had already begun to blossom. The sick man lay observing these drops. They served as a kind of rosary . . . The idea came to him, struck a part of his consciousness, that the hour of his death was drawing near. Behind him lay a life that was no better and no worse than other lives; he had loved, suffered, traveled, and written. Many people thought, and had said as much in articles, especially after his eightieth birthday, that his life had been filled with work and solitude. But no one knew the price of this work, in terms of renunciation, or how it was as forced as it was beneficial. He recalled, "as if through a foggy mist" (as a refined stylist he certainly never would have used this phrase), that he had been through some terrible crises in recent days, that he had resisted death with all his might, that he had avoided its clutches, that he had torn the tubes out of his veins and spit into death's face, and that he had wept as he struggled with the phantom of death that was invisible but present; sometimes it stood by his bed and sometimes it was inside him, in his intestines, in his lungs, and in his feverish mind.

And then, on that morning—he knew neither when nor how— the calm descended. He accepted the unacceptable: for him it was all over. His days, his hours were numbered. He made an attempt to take stock of how he had lived, seeing his life from the others' points of view, and it made him chuckle to himself. He was going to die, therefore, having filled up his life with solitude, self-abnegation, and labor; *for all human endeavors teach but this one thing: that the meaning of human activity on earth resides in law, moderation, order, and renunciation. And everything great and beautiful that is made, is made with blood or sweat, and in silence.* Who had said that? Had he read it somewhere or perhaps even written it himself? But the point was that, at this time, this thought seemed to him at the very least accurate, if not all too comforting.

He thought how nice it would be to have at his side one of those noble and sage individuals whom he had come to know over the course of his life: Alaupović, or Mr. Ivo Vojnović . . . In his lifetime he had met only two or three people as wise as they. The rest were like the majority of the human race: narrow-minded and selfish, with no sense of beauty, lacking sympathy for others, ignorant. They were people guided only by instinct and ambition—for love and food, for fame and fleeting glory. And whenever they entered his life, they created disorder, like an army occupying a city.

He looked at himself with others' eyes and took stock of his life as the others, the strangers, saw it: he was leaving behind his collected works, in which his biography, his language, stood mingled with the history of his nation; this guaranteed him the thing people call immortality. Among his papers there were still a few texts that he kept, painstakingly sorted and selected, in bundles: poems, journals, notes. He had removed from these manuscripts everything that could have compromised him in the eyes of posterity, every trace of personal life, every private item, so that he would remain, in the eyes of future generations, even more of an abstraction, even more a writer, but less of a man of flesh of blood. There was, in this gesture of his, something both bitter and just: after all, he had spent all his days in the domain of fiction, in the world of Platonic ideals, and every side-trip he'd made into life turned into torment and misfortune, embarrassment and monotony. Every real-life decision outside the world of pure ideas, beyond the quiet and solitude, had brought him only injury; every action had missed the mark, every encounter with others had proved a setback, and every success was only a fresh misfortune. So he removed all names other than his own from those texts. He removed this entire ephemeral world that could only besmirch his name: because proving a fool to be a fool amounts to compromising oneself.

Then the thought flashed abruptly through his mind, like an electric shock extending deep into his core, that he had not paid off his debts. Not the spiritual but the earthly ones. (As for the spiritual debts, not a single person has ever paid them back to anyone: not to God nor one's own mother, neither to one's language nor one's homeland.) No, he wasn't thinking of those debts; he'd be taking them along with him into that other world. (And if that world truly exists, if there really is a reason for it to exist, then it is precisely this: for a person to pay back his creditors.) He was simply thinking of the kind of debts that one can settle with money, even if only in a symbolic way, like a word of greeting, a handshake, now that he could no longer postpone this any further, now that the time had come to settle up with this world. Even the modest subvention—of two hundred crowns—that was provided to him by the Croatian "Progress" society and that reached him every month without fail (something that was a genuine miracle in these turbulent times and was a real credit to those Habsburg institutions, whatever else people thought of them) had to be parsed sensibly, distributed wisely: so that everybody benefited from it and no one was wronged.

He watched as the drops bulged in the bottle fastened over his head, and he counted them, one by one, the way one counts the beads of a rosary, or gold coins.

To Ivan Matkovšek, the *Wachtmeister*, who opened my eyes to landscapes, the way a soldier learns to read terrain from a map: two crowns.

To Ajkuna Hreljić, the first person to take my hand and lead me across the bridge: two crowns.

To Ana Matkovšek, who taught me the language of flowers and herbs: two crowns.

To Draginja Trifković, the schoolteacher, who taught me my first letters of the alphabet: two crowns.

To Idriz Azizović, nicknamed "the Arab," who taught me how to listen to the human voice, which can be a musical instrument: two crowns.

To Ljubomir Popović, who taught me kindness, because it isn't enough simply to have a kind heart, and goodness has to be learned like the alphabet: two crowns.

To Milan Gavrilović, who taught me friendship, because friendship also has to be learned like a foreign language: two crowns.

To Ratko Bogdanović, who taught me that friendship is not sufficient, since even it can be selfish: two crowns.

To Jovan Vasić, schoolteacher, who encouraged me when I needed bravery to take the path of literature: two crowns.

To Tugomir Alaupović, who watched over my soul and my body as he did his very own: two crowns.

To Mijo Poljak, professor, who enabled me to read German, which was most useful throughout my life and furnished me with intellectual diversion: two crowns.

To Dimitrije Mitrinović, who revealed to me the existence of other worlds, better and happier, beyond these hapless provincial backwaters: two crowns.

To Vladimir Gaćinović, who uncovered for me that region of the world and the soul that is like unto the dark side of the moon: two crowns.

To Bogdan Žerajić, who poisoned me with doubt about the worth of words, leading me to regard them with distrust and weigh them out one by one, as if they were gold pieces: two crowns.

To Fanika and Evgenija Gojmerac, who poisoned me with music and love; but music and love—they are like twin sisters holding hands . . . one of them playing a *polonaise* by Chopin and the other kindling the holy fire of love in me with her poems and letters . . . for in the beginning was love: four crowns.

A drop had separated from the bottle, and another now started to well up in its place. That's fitting, he thought. That one was about two people, so each deserves a bead of the rosary; each deserves a memory.

To Milan Rešetar, Jozef Jireček, Vilhelm Jeruzalem, Oskar Evald, Jozef Klem, my professors, who taught me that knowledge is everything, while ignorance begets fanaticism and spiritual darkness: ten crowns.

To Doctor Oskar Aleksander, laryngologist from Ilica Street, who operated on my throat after explaining to me in advance the point of the surgical procedure and who treated me like a human being, not a sheep: two crowns.

To the waiter in the "Green Salon" in Krakow, who served me herbal tea the way I like it, and the way the state of my health requires, and who did so gladly and with a smile: two crowns.

To Helena Iržikovski, who instructed me in the deciphering of the "divine hieroglyphics"—musical notes—so that I wouldn't stand there, dumb as an ox, before this Gothic architecture in lyrical form: two crowns.

To Jan Loc Nepomucen, who disclosed to me the fact that upon the magnificent tree of languages every bird sings in its own way, and that our preferences for certain languages are every bit as individual, arbitrary, and mysterious as our choices in love: two crowns.

To Marjan Zdjehovski, who laid bare for me the deep roots of that Slavic linguistic tree from which branched off the languages of Pushkin, Słowacki, Murn, and my "Bosnian," too: two crowns.

To Maja Nižetić and Jerko Čulić, to whom I became indebted for gifts, words, and favors during my prison term: four crowns.

To the unfortunate Vladimir Čerini, who gave me a thousand *dinars* when I needed it the most, and who gave it "anonymously," so to speak, so that the recipient, who was in trouble, did not perceive it as charity or a humiliation: two crowns.

To the unknown guard at the prison in Maribor, who pushed a scrap of paper and a tiny pencil under my door when writing meant survival for me: two crowns.

To the judge from Split, Jerko Moskovito, who assisted me in regaining my freedom at my trial, and who thereby demonstrated the degree to which one's personal attitude and courage in hard times are capable of changing that fate which cowards believe to be inevitable and pronounce to be fate or historical necessity: two crowns.

To Fr. Alojzije Perčinlić, who revealed to me the strict, penurious, and industrious life of Franciscan monks; had I not become a "poet," I would have become a priest: two crowns.

To Stipica Lukić, a Franciscan novice, who brought me bread, belief, and hope in the prison at Zenica: two crowns.

To the honorable sisters Hermina and Eparhija, who showed me by their example how one can subordinate the body to spiritual concerns, something that I tried to apply to my own life, within the limits of my own modest powers: four crowns.

To Count Ivo Vojnović, my benefactor and Maecenas, who saw in me that which I myself had hoped to possess: talent, that divinely bestowed blessing and curse: two crowns.

To Mr. Dinko Lukšić from Sutivan, whose hospitality made my days more pleasant and improved my health so that I could complete my volume of poetry: two crowns.

To the young investigating magistrate, a Viennese, who, on the occasion of my arrest in Split, allowed me to send for my personal effects, which had remained behind in my pension; he brought me Kierkegaard's *Either/Or*, and that book would end up having a decisive impact on my intellect: two crowns.

To the sentry who allowed me to retrieve this book from the prison warehouse, where they kept the items they confiscated from us: two crowns.

To Jaromir Studnjički, the bookseller and bibliophile from Sarajevo, who exposed me to the "cosmic light" of books: two crowns.

To Gospava Dunđerović, who knew how to tell stories from the Ottoman times in the way the bards with their *guslas* once did— *drawn out, lovely, precise*: two crowns.

To Luj Bakotić, who made it possible for me not to squander my time in Rome on office work and for me not to be weighed down by obligations, so that instead I was able to learn, observe, and write: two crowns.

("At the end, at the real final end, everything is good and everything is resolved harmoniously." That's Ivo Andrić. From *Days of the Consuls*.)

To Vladislav Budisavljević, whose understanding made it possible for me to devote myself to writing and to the study of history: in my work, these two things are mingled and interlaced, so that one can't tell where the one begins and the other ceases: two crowns.

To Mrs. Vera Stojić, who took care of my manuscripts and correspondence, doing so out of love and respect: two crowns.

To Midhad Šamić, who discovered my sources and interpreted them in terms of erudition and creative impotence: one crown.

To that professor who gave me a copy of his book of aphorisms for my birthday: a crown (although actually he should give me a crown for having read it). As the old adage goes, a loan oft loses both itself and friend.

To Nurse Olga, who takes care of me, and who puts fresh flowers in my vase every morning and turns me over in my bed with a light but careful touch.

And on he went counting like that, to himself, in the quiet of the room filled with artificial light like the evening sun. At first his thoughts followed a chronology, but with the mounting pain (there wasn't anything specific that ached; rather, everything caused him pain, and life itself hurt) the order became jumbled, the events grew confused, and time lost its way; only now and again did a coherent thought surface, as when the sun plays hide and seek behind the clouds.

He attempted, using his rosary of insulin drops, a rosary like those made of pearls, to tot up all the many sums he had enumerated so that he could establish the total amount he owed. He would begin and then stop again, then start counting once more with a vague dread, a dread akin to a shudder, that his woeful stipend—of two hundred crowns—would not be enough. He would have to leave somebody out for now; leave them empty-handed; he would have to remain indebted to someone. But whom should he cross off the list, especially when this list comprised only a part of his debts? He tried to reduce the total, to distribute it differently, but at any rate it wasn't a sum of money that was at issue. Rather it was a sign of consideration, the result of his wish not to remain indebted to anyone in this world, at least insofar as one can settle accounts uniformly with one's relatives, creditors, benefactors, and nuisances.

The nurse was sitting in the adjacent room, and through the open door she kept an eye on the monitor where the functions of the patient's heart were being charted in jagged but evenly spaced waves. In her starched white smock, and with a white ribbon in her hair, she sat sideways at a table, reading a romance novel in *Bazaar* magazine: she was riding along on the wide blacktop; next to her sat Nick Chester with his shirt unbuttoned to reveal his powerful, hairy chest. "Nick had laid his right hand on her taut thigh; the car glided noiselessly along the broad asphalt road in the direction of Colorado. But suddenly, when he turned his head toward her to say those words she had waited so long to hear . . ." The nurse braced herself by pressing her orthopedic sandals against the wall with all her might, as if to prevent the catastrophe that was taking shape in the next line of the text, in the form of a huge eighteen-wheeler; the truck appeared out of a curve and its headlights blinded Nick Chester, who never even got around to uttering the words that his young heart was dictating to him. Glancing up from the pages of *Bazaar*, where love was being extinguished before her eyes, the nurse directed her sleepy, mournful gaze at the monitor: the waves were growing ever more jagged and a glowing dot, accompanied by a light beep, was skipping across the white horizontal line. It was like the screen of a ping-pong video game (which she had seen two years before in a hotel down in Budva).

Then her eyes fell upon the sick man, and it seemed to her that he was moving his lips. Knowing that this was an important patient, she abandoned her spot on the seat of the Cadillac for a moment, there to the right of Nick Chester, and went over to the bed.

The patient looked her straight in the eyes.

"Do you need anything?"

"Lend me two crowns."

His words were quiet, labored, but perfectly intelligible.

"Excuse me," the nurse said, leaning over closer to him. "I didn't quite get that."

"I am two crowns shy of being able to settle my debts. I won't stay indebted to you either, Nurse. I don't want to remain indebted to anyone. I'll pay it all back to you, too, right down to the last *kreuzer*."

"Of course. I know you're good for it. I'll bring you the money right away."

At that point she went over to the adjoining room.

"Doctor, the patient in No. 5 is asking me to lend him two crowns."

"Give them to him, Nurse."

"But two *crowns*, sir?"

"His mind is wandering, Nurse. Give him two *dinars*. If his condition worsens, call me. As long as he's quiet, I don't want to go in. That might upset him. Go. Do you have the two *dinars*?"

"Yes," said the nurse, taking her change purse out of the pocket of her apron.

"Here you go," the nurse said as she laid the coins on the nightstand next to the patient's bed; they vibrated on the marble top and then the noise abruptly stopped.

"Doctor! Doctor!" the nurse called out. "He's stopped breathing. Look at the monitor. His heart's stopped beating."

"Summon the director quickly," said the doctor. "You, Nurse, you paid the fare for his ride on Charon's ferry."

A AND B

A

(*The magical place*)

From Kotor (Kotor is located in the Zeta region of Yugoslavia, on the Gulf of Cattaro, a bay off the Adriatic) you must set out at around five in the morning. After an hour of driving up the steep serpentine curves, you have to stop somewhere and wait.

The day must be clear, but there have to be a few white clouds in the west that are reminiscent of a herd of white elephants.

Then you have to let your eyes take in the sea, the mountains, the sky.

And then the sky, the mountains, the sea.

And you have to know for certain that your father traveled this same stretch of road, either on a bus or in a taxi he had hired in Kotor, and you have to be convinced that he beheld this same sight: the sun popping into view in the west from behind clouds that looked like a herd of white elephants; the high mountains dissolving in mist; the inky dark blue of the water in the bay; the city at the foot of the mountains; the white ship putting in at the jetty; the soap factory where thick smoke gushed into the air from chimneys and enormous windows glowed with fiery light.

You also have to take note of those chirping crickets (as if a million wristwatches were being wound up), for they are otherwise so easily forgotten, the same way it's possible not to notice, because of its omnipresence, the smell of sagebrush at the side of the road.

Then the thing is to forget everything else, and to observe from this godlike vantage point the meeting of the elements: air, earth, water.

If all of these conditions are met, you will acquire an experience of eternity that Koestler called "oceanic feeling."

PS:

A friend of mine, a press photographer, took pictures, with the permission of the captain, on board a Soviet cruiser that had anchored at Kotor. Afterward, from land, he photographed with a wide lens the ship and the landscape around the bay. When he developed the film, it was as black as night.

The awareness of eternity, the "oceanic feeling," yielded, independent of any technique of *brouillage*, only blots, red, black, or green, insofar as the senses of hearing, smell, and sight were unavailable during the taking of the photographs.

My father viewed this same scene in 1939 (five years before he disappeared at Auschwitz) and in 1898 so did Mr. Sigmund Freud, who went on to have his famous dream about the three Fates.

B

(The worst rathole I visited?)

From outside:

The house is obscured on one side by the village administrative building, on the other by a wooden stable, and on the front side by a short beech tree. The house is made of dried mud, the room of darkened tiles that have shattered or slipped in places. The door is small, so that a grown person can enter only by bending at the waist. A window, half a square meter in size, looks out onto the tree, which stands at a distance of about ten meters from the shack. This window opens outward. On the other side, facing the "garden," where the outhouse is located, along with a neglected tract of untilled land, overgrown with weeds, there is a round opening for light built directly into the wall. The pane on it is partially broken and the hole is plugged up with rags.

From inside:

The space is divided by a thin mudded wall: the bigger side measures 2 m x 2 m, the smaller one 2 m x 1 m. The first one is called a "bedroom," the second one a "kitchen." The walls have been whitewashed with an ochre-colored preparation made by dissolving clay in lukewarm water. The effects of dampness and sunshine are such that this coating blisters or develops cracks that look like scales or the faded canvases of Old Masters. The floor is also of pounded clay that lies several centimeters lower than the surface of the yard. On humid days the clay smells of urine. (A shed for animals once stood here.)

In the larger room there are two wooden bed frames and two chests of drawers that are pulled out twenty to thirty centimeters from the wall. A rag carpet is stretched diagonally across the floor from the entranceway to the kitchen. In a corner of the kitchen stands a stove made of sheet metal. Two or three pots hang on heavy nails, and a wooden trunk serves as a sleeping platform and a pantry. Next to the stove lies a pile of decaying wet spruce cones for heating. There's thick smoke in the kitchen, so thick that the people who sit on the chest or on the short wooden stools can barely see. Their voices work their way through the smoke as through water.

"Here was the alarm clock. On this nail," I say to the man who brought me here in a car from Budapest. "A drunken Russian sailor took it in 1945."

"Someday there will be a plaque here," the man noted ironically as we were leaving the house. "It will say: HERE LIVED THE YU-GOSLAV WRITER DANILO KIŠ FROM 1942 TO 1945."

"Fortunately, the house is slated to be torn down," I say.

"That's a shame," said the man who had brought me here in a car from Budapest. "If I had a camera with me, I'd take some pictures of it."

PS:

Texts A and B are connected to each other by mysterious bonds.

THE MARATHON RUNNER
AND THE RACE OFFICIAL

Although it does not entirely make sense in terms of chronology, I am convinced that it was from the late Leonid Šejka, the painter who referred to himself also as a "classifier," that I first heard this story. Whether he read Abram Tertz's book in manuscript form or someone related the story to him verbally, I do not know. But at any rate I'm sure that it was he who first recounted it to me. (He followed the winded runners with his eyes as they jockeyed for position, in the grip of terrible corporeal and mental strain amid an imaginary landscape to which he gave form and color. With three fingers of his right hand pressed together for emphasis, he sought the correct word and the right expression as if testing with the tips of his fingers the smoothness of a pigment or the thickness of a coat of paint; meanwhile his hand remained immobile, strangely still, as if paralyzed: in it a cigarette burns slowly while its ash remains intact, vertical.)

Here's the story:

The marathon runners are warming up for the race in their shorts and tank tops to which bibs with large numbers are affixed. Among them were some who were participating for the first time, but there were also seasoned champions there, as well as one tall bony man, fifty years old, who was a celebrated veteran of many races and a winner many times over in the past, the pride of his nation.

It's early autumn or late spring. Above the main square, a banner inscribed with the word "Start" stretches from the baroque town hall to a building housing a restaurant. Ladies are coming out of morning Mass, leading by the hands little boys with carefully combed hair. Young women in long skirts and lace collars are chatting gaily, their white gloves still in place.

When the race official lowers his flag, the runners take off with feigned unconcern. They have twenty-five kilometers in front of them, and even the neophytes know that they aren't supposed to put their bodies and minds into high gear until much later.

And thus off they go, all bunched together, through the streets of the city that are in some places exposed to the sun (at which they pull their visors down over their eyes) and in other places through great polygons of shade, where tall buildings block the light. Office denizens take up positions on the sidewalks and applaud irresolutely; gentlemen brandish their canes, pointing out their favorites; the hairdressers abandon their lathered-up customers for a few minutes; and the apprentices, leaning on their doorposts, follow with a look of nostalgia in their eyes those lucky ones to whom fate has granted a freedom as good as wings, and to one of whom will belong the glorious status of victor.

They are still running in a pack, and through the thinning applause they can hear only the rhythmic scraping of their shoes and their own breathing. Then the city gradually falls behind them.

They pass the smoke-filled slums, the paper mill, and the brewery; the train depot was on their left; now they have crossed the bridge; this is where the fields begin, and the meadows and the thickets of reeds from which the morning sun causes mist and the smell of grass to rise. This smell compels them to press their eyes shut as if the divine power of nature, the Antaeus-like juices of the earth, might thereby flow more easily into lungs and blood through their straining breath.

The route is marked off with flags, and the motorcycle, sputtering and meandering in front of them, prevents the runners from losing their way. Meanwhile, the compact mass of runners has broken up. Of course at first this is still just a test of their strength or whatever early (and temporary) crises they might experience before the bodies subordinate themselves to the power of will and reason and ambition; or until they give out completely.

Valdemar D., wearing #25, a tall fellow about thirty years of age, with close-cropped blond hair and long, lean legs, felt how he had finally shaken off his body's lassitude, and by the time he reached the edge of the woods, he felt he had likewise overcome the sluggishness in his muscles, the indifference of his bones, the laziness of the soles of his feet—and at last overpowered this animal of a body that a saint had once named his donkey. He ran easily and his legs felt fresh, moving like well-oiled pistons. As if the forest smells and the redolent conifers had given him new strength. The sound of chainsaws, the hammering of axe-blows on sonorous tree trunks, the aroma of moist sawdust, reminiscent of urine— these were all distant echoes of his childhood.

Notwithstanding the agreement with his trainer, now faded and forgotten in his mind, he picked up the pace on a downhill stretch in the woods in what would have been a respectable end-of-race kick, and he worked his way up to the front of the group that was in the lead; the famous veteran was in this group, running as an honorary competitor in his valedictory race. For a moment it seemed to the marathon runner that the veteran was looking at him in bewilderment, and then the veteran shook his head as if to make it clear that this was not the way to do things. It was not yet time to go for the lead since they had just barely cleared the city: the tolling of the bells from the municipal bell tower could still clearly be heard.

When he came out into open country, Valdemar D. turned around. Behind him he saw the green barrier of the woods and the narrow path, empty of people. (He imagined the others on their way up the last incline deep in the heart of the forest, panting, and finding his footprints in the mud.)

He knew the lay of the land around here, knew it very well indeed; he'd had the good fortune of training on this same path along which he was now hurtling, propelled by the bracing wind and a sense of rapture that he had long ago forgotten.

At the six-kilometer mark they splashed a can of water on his face; at seven kilometers someone handed him a bottle and as he ran he drank the liquid that smelled of elderberry and tasted like rainwater; at ten kilometers somebody shouted that he should slow his pace and save his strength for the finish; in the eleventh kilometer he sank up to his ankles in the muck hard by a lake.

With the astonishment of someone skilled and well-trained—a seasoned runner who had started off with short distances until he found his real niche, aided by the advice of his coach, in long-distance events where the role of luck is reduced to the absolute minimum but will-power, experience, and preparation are decisive—he realized that he was running the race of his life, that he would win the trophy that hundreds or even thousands of athletes yearned for. Ecstatic at the fact that his body was obeying him without effort or opposition, he attained complete harmony with this corporeal instrument; having broken its resistance, having conquered and subjugated it, he reflected on the biological miracle that had enabled him to overwhelm the inertia of his body, the resistance of matter and gravity—and he thought about how he had succeeded, in the manner of an Indian fakir, to adjust the function of his heart, to control its rhythm. He wondered how this magical harmony, this ideal balancing act of will, strength, years, and days had come to be.

And now he turned around, but in vain. Behind him were nothing but gently rolling green hills, forested heights, and the red reflection of the lake; not a visual clue or a sound connected with the people in whose company he began this race.

The sun, passing along its high arc, was his only accompaniment.

The shiny cross on the village steeple grew ever nearer. From the slates leaning against trees along the route, he followed the passage of the kilometers until he finally discovered, not without amazement, that on one of them—propped up against a telegraph pole—was written the number twelve. A record time even for a five thousand-meter race, he thought, and his heart was filled with joy, a joy that frightened him a little, as if he were witnessing some wondrous and unknown phenomenon bordering on the superhuman, the impossible. For if he felt this fresh here, at the half-way point, then it was only some unexpected misfortune, an awkward fall or a wrenched ankle, that could prevent him from setting a fantastic record that would go down in the annals of sports. A triumph worthy of the Marathon myth.

On the edge of the next village, the motorcycle slowed down and pulled into a soccer field overgrown with grass and tall weeds. (The sound of the motor died out abruptly and he thought it must have broken down.) There he saw someone next to the decrepit goalposts beckoning with a little yellow flag. He turned around, thinking the signal wasn't meant for him but rather for some boys who had been trailing him, or for some inquisitive cyclist who had gotten too close. But there was no one behind him. The motorcycle curved around and stopped right by the goal. The driver pushed his rubber goggles up onto his forehead and stretched his arms out in a gesture of helplessness.

Valdemar D. looked closely at the race official and had the feeling he knew this man from somewhere; he seemed to recognize the short brawny arms, the bowlegs, the massive squarish head. The umpire kept waving the flag and indicated by his energetic remonstrations that the marathoner was to stop running.

"Number 25, you must take a breather," he heard the judge's voice saying. (Even this voice somehow seemed familiar to him.)

Valdemar D. kept running anyway, looking for a way out of this neglected, weed-covered soccer field. On all sides, a fence of rusty barbed wire. Valdemar D. knew that he couldn't stop, that he couldn't stop *now*, now that he had achieved what he had achieved, now that he'd covered half the course. So he kept on running, round and round in circles riding his momentum so the machine of his body wouldn't get winded, so that his flywheel would not come to a halt, so his body's mechanisms wouldn't grind down, so his forward motion wouldn't diminish, so the rhythm of his stride and his heart wouldn't be disrupted. Hardly out of breath at all, he called to the race official (my God, he knew that head from somewhere):

"Sir, I'm not tired."

And he kept running, around and around in circles.

"I command you to stop and catch your breath!" the race official screamed at him, his face beet red; he waved the flag up and down, up and down. "That's an order!"

Valdemar called back to him over his shoulder, without breaking his stride:

"But, sir, if I stop now . . ."

"You must stop this instant, Number 25. I order you to halt! Did you hear me? Knock it off!"

"At the half-way mark?" Valdemar groaned, continuing to run and looking in vain for a passage through the rusty wire.

"It's for your own good," the umpire shouted, forgetting for a moment to wave the little flag. "If you don't believe me, No. 25, here's a person here who will convince you that it's in your best interests. You are tired."

At that point Maria appeared from the tent at a sign from the official. (This low-ceilinged tent apparently served as a command post, and it was equipped with a field telephone.) He recognized her even before she began to speak, although her straw hat covered half her face with its shadow.

"Valdemar," she shouted to him. She was scared of something, "I implore you to stop! Come, take a rest. You *must* rest, Valdemar!"

Then he woke up. The dream crumbled like the stack of ashes on the end of a long-burning cigarette. Waking up felt like a fall, like the fall of an angel. Had he not been ranging through paradise itself just a short while ago? Maria, whose voice still resounded clearly in his mind, had been dead—to keep this in some sort of coherent perspective—for more than fifteen years.

Outside the day was dawning, dirty and gray.

There was still enough time to tell his dream to the man lying next to him in the bunk of this Siberian labor camp. After Valdemar's sudden death, however, the latter man told the story to another prisoner who is also now dead. Thus Valdemar's dream reached Abram Tertz, who used to tell his wife all sorts of things in his letters. The camp censor scarcely paid any attention to Tertz's letters anymore, since he carried on like an idiot in them and was more likely to write about God, the devil, and Gogol than about the weather, diarrhea, and the lousy *makhorka*.

Tertz concluded the story of the unfortunate man from Latvia with this laconic comment (in this letter to his wife he still needed to save space for Providence and Gogol's nose): "He had precisely 12 years and 6 months to go before the end of his sentence." On the next page (p. 76) of the London edition, he added, in a separate context and yet somewhat paradoxically: "Sleep is the watering place of the soul to which it hastens at night to drink at the sources of life."

Recently, while reading the book by Tertz, I remembered Šejka's story. (I am more and more convinced that he had to have had a copy of the manuscript.) He narrated the course of events in his own way, referring frequently to Berdyaev, Dostoyevsky, and Beckett. He was lonely, sick, and Russian. And he knew how to bathe his story in the same mysterious light that emanated from his paintings.

TRANSLATOR'S AFTERWORD

Danilo Kiš (1935–1989) remains best known in his native Serbia and in the world of translation as a novelist. If one throws into his dossier the fact that his fiction was mildly (and bravely) postmodern and that the Holocaust was one of his main themes, we will have just about reached the end of our popular, journalistic understanding of the man and his works. Yet the refinement, even the reframing, of Kiš's profile continues as we move well into the third decade following his premature death of lung cancer in Paris. Recent years have seen the publication of more and more scholarly articles about the methods and themes of his works, as well as the translations of some additional stories, an early novel, and a play; in Serbia there are even new primary sources coming to light, such as the two Kiš film scripts, published in late 2011 as *Dva filmska scenarija*, and the occasional rebroadcast of his 1989 collection of filmed interviews in Israel with "double victims" of fascism and (early) Yugoslav communism, *Goli život* (Bare Life). The new trends arising from this publishing activity—trends that supplement but in no way supplant the basic Western critical understanding of Kiš originating in his "family cycle" of novels and stories and in the carefully selected, cosmopolitan essays brought out in the English-language version of *Homo Poeticus* during the war-torn 1990s—could arguably be summed up as increased attention both to the Yugoslav milieu depicted in his writings and to his artistic and ethical aversion to Stalinism. There are a number of other jewels awaiting their turn to speak to audiences in translation, and Kiš's life itself still awaits a great biography, in any language. The publication of this volume is, in my opinion, a bracing new chapter in Serbian and East European literature, and . . . one might add . . . it represents only a fraction of the excellent work that still remains inaccessible in English.

The seven stories contained in this version of *The Lute and the Scars* do not have an overarching common theme. They do, however, all very much bear the stamp of the author's mind and touch. They are enjoyable, by turns intimate and politically obstreperous and sad and even funny, and their diversity will allow a fuller appreciation of Kiš's thematic concerns and, possibly, his stylistic approaches. One of the stories, "The Stateless One," reflects themes explored elsewhere in Kiš's oeuvre—here, the difficult relationship of an artist to his work and skepticism about modern nationalism—though, even so, it is unique in choosing a (real) late Habsburg novelist as its protagonist. "Jurij Golec" is a touching and elegiac treatment of the last days and legacy of a Soviet refugee writer in Paris; it is without doubt one of this translator's favorite stories in the volume, by dint of its alternating tones of sadness and levity, as well as its serving as a reminder of the existence of a little-known Holocaust novel, Piotr Rawicz's

Blood from the Sky, which ranks alongside key works by Aharon Appelfeld, David Grossman, Aleksandar Tišma, and Kiš himself among the indispensable fictional treatments of Nazi genocide. "Jurij Golec" is also the cosmopolitan equivalent of the very Yugoslav and very political account of a man of letters driven to desperation by ideological and physical brutalization at the hands of the secret police that we find in "The Poet." Also rooted firmly in the Serbian context, and beautifully and humanely demonstrating Kiš's respect for Nobel Prize-winner Ivo Andrić, for whom he had enormous but seldom discussed admiration, is "The Debt," a stream-of-consciousness final will and testament of the great writer in his final days in the hospital. "A and B" is a short but challenging autobiographical essay that condenses many of Kiš's unconventional views about the "brutality" of Central Europe and the nobility of the Balkans (an inversion of the typical epithets); this is also the thematic register of his great novels *Garden, Ashes* and *Hourglass*. Finally, "The Lute and the Scars" is another colorful autobiographical piece that depicts bohemian Belgrade in the 1950s, the cold, lingering Stalinism of the USSR, and the struggle of a young writer to find authenticity and maintain personal integrity. "The Marathon Runner and the Race Official," also bearing the imprint of inimical Soviet conditions, memorializes the precariousness—the mortal condition of being pitilessly "exposed," if you will—of the marginalized and marked outsider: Kiš's preferred formula for the concept of "victim." Each of these stories is anchored in Kiš's biography or in literary history more generally.

For an overview of the complicated genesis of the stories in this volume, the following table has been assembled from the original notes provided in the Serbian edition.

STORY	WRITTEN	PUBL. DATE
The Stateless One	c. 1980	1992
Jurij Golec	c. 1982	1994
The Lute and the Scars	1983	1993
The Poet	c. 1983	c. 1994
The Debt	1986	1992
A and B	1986	1990
The Marathon Runner and the Race Official	1982	1995

Readers will perhaps find it useful to stay attuned, while immersed in these stories, to conceptions of "home," to various ways of embodying and depicting the "creative life," and to the corrosive effects of dystopian dictatorships. The stories do at times have a lyricism that approaches the inimitable writing in the stories of *Early Sorrows: For Children and Sensitive Readers*; they are, on the other hand, nowhere near as bloody as, and by and large not as harrowing as, the stupendous component tales of *A Tomb for Boris Davidovich*. They have enough of the virtues of these other story collections to elicit a strong reaction from readers, however, and they also read like "vintage Kiš": to wit, the compression, the enumeration, the poignant detail, and the restlessly conversational language. The stories also offer us a chance to embrace a more fully Yugoslav, or Serbian, Kiš. The deep affection for Ivo Andrić and, metaphorically, the acknowledgement of the author's own set of "debts," is every bit as much "the real Kiš" as the cosmopolitanism—an artist's search for authenticity and intuitive acceptance of diversity and intellectual and emotional (as opposed to political or ethnic) affinity—of "The Stateless One." Likewise, the reflections on Yugoslav conditions in "The Lute and the Scars" and in this translator's other favorite story in the collection, "The Poet," are just as real as his many nonfiction pieces on French symbolism, Thomas Mann, and James Joyce. Finally, the looming presence of the USSR in so many of these stories reminds us that the political coloration of the backdrop to Kiš's life changed, significantly, from black to red before his teenage years were out. This epic turn left its indelible marks on his intellectual biography, and it precipitated neatly into that most engaging of his plays, *Night and Fog* (see *Absinthe: New European Writing* 12 [2009]: 94–133).

* * *

These stories are deceptively complex, and their publication history is also complex. Therefore they received a good and necessary measure of critical attention and analysis as they were published—hence the indispensability of notes in and on the tales themselves. The original published notes to the stories can be found at the end of this volume.

The basis for the translations of the first six stories is the collection *Lauta i ožiljci*, edited by Mirjana Miočinovič and published by the Beogradski izdavački-grafički zavod (BIGZ) in Belgrade in 1994. For the provenance of the final story in this collection, "The Marathon Runner and the Race Official," please see the notes at the end of the book.

I owe a debt of real thanks to the following friends for their help with various aspects of these translations: Predrag and Tamara Apić, Jessica Blissit, Sara Brown, Pascale Delpech, Ken Goldwasser, Bea and Wolfgang Klotz, John McLaughlin, Dragan Miljković, Mirjana Miočinović, Jeff Pennington, Dan Shea, Predrag Stokić, Aleksandar Štulhofer, Verena Theile, Gary Totten, and Milo Yelesiyevich. From books and encouragement to food, friendship, and fine points of vocabulary, these wonderful people have made bringing stories by Kiš to an anglophone audience into a very satisfying adventure.

This book is dedicated to the memory of Murlin Croucher. He was a mentor to many of us in the field of East European and Russian studies, an accomplished librarian, a universal wit and seeker, one pug-crazy dude, a lover of great literature wherever it was to be found, and my friend since 1987. *Requiescat in pacem.*

JOHN K. COX, 2012

NOTES TO THE ORIGINAL EDITION

Original Notes

These explanatory notes, a kind of critical apparatus for the individual stories in this collection, were written and first published by Mirjana Miočinović. The vast majority of them have been translated from the first edition of Lauta i ožiljci (published in 1994 by BIGZ in Beograd). There are four exceptions to this attribution. The last sentence in the entry for "The Lute and the Scars" and the final three paragraphs of the entry for "The Poet" are additions taken from the 1995 edition of Skladište. In the notes to "The Debt," the comparative material on Eugène Ionesco is also from Skladište. The entire entry for "The Marathon Runner and the Race Official," like the beginning and end of the story itself, was taken from the subsequently published French and German editions of the story, since I have not yet seen a Serbian edition. —JKC

General Remarks

The stories from Kiš's literary estate entitled "The Stateless One," "Jurij Golec," "The Lute and the Scars," "The Poet," and "The Debt," all of which we are bringing out in this volume, originated in the years between 1980 and 1986, connected more or less directly with the book *The Encyclopedia of the Dead*. We have supplemented these with the short two-part prose piece "A and B," which in manuscript form had no title. Although it does not seem to fit the definition of "short fiction," it does function in a metaphoric (and metonymic) way in relation to the larger body of Kiš's work in prose: hence its place in this collection, and its position at the end, as a sort of "lyric epilogue."

The stories "Jurij Golec" and "The Poet" are being published here for the first time. The others have already been published in this order: "A and B" in the book *Život, literatura* (Svjetlost, Sarajevo, 1990); "The Stateless One" in *Srpski književni glasnik* (1992, vol. 1); "The Debt" in *Književne novine* (1992, pp. 850–851); and "The Lute and the Scars" in *Nedeljna borba* (April 30–May 5, 1993).

In giving to this book the title *The Lute and the Scars*, we were guided by the fact that Kiš named two of his three collections of stories after one of the collected tales themselves; he did so less because of the story's privileged position in its collection than because of the ability of the title itself to bring thematic unity to the other stories. It seemed to us that we could accomplish something similar with this title, in addition to enjoying its inherently paradoxical quality.

The Stateless One

The story "The Stateless One," which comes down to us in "incomplete and imperfect" form, was inspired by the life of Ödön von Horváth. It will not be difficult for the reader to comprehend the reasons for Kiš's interest in this "Central European fate" that ended in such a bizarre manner on the Champs-Élysées on the eve of the Second World War: Ödön von Horváth died on June 1, 1938, during a storm that descended abruptly on Paris, obliterating trees and sweeping away everything in its path. A heavy branch took Ödön von Horváth's life, right in front of the doors to the Théâtre Marigny. He had arrived in Paris after an encounter with a "premium fortune-teller" in Amsterdam, who had prophesied that an event awaited him in the French capital that would fundamentally alter his life! (It is also easy to recognize the figure of an unnamed poet who plays an indirect but important role in this story: Endre Ady, whose life and literary fate was intertwined in similar ways with those of both Horváth and Kiš. In this sense, "The Stateless One" is in some of its passages a condensed replica of parts of Kiš's story "An Excursion to Paris," which dates from 1959 and was dedicated to Ady.)

Kiš first obtained translations of some of Horváth's plays in 1970. These were the French versions that Gallimard published in 1967 (namely *Italian Night, Don Juan Comes Back from the War,* and *Tales from the Vienna Woods*), prepared with an introduction that provided French readers with basic information about the life of this writer who had been utterly unknown up to that point. At this point Horváth began appearing in Kiš's "warehouse" of emblematic figures and "themes for novels, topics for stories, parallels . . ." But ten years would have to pass (this was the decade in which he wrote *Hourglass*, *A Tomb for Boris Davidovich*, and *The Anatomy Lesson*) before the fate of this *stateless man*, which was attractive for reasons far exceeding mere literary interest, would again come to the front of Kiš's mind. For it was in 1979 that Kiš began his ten-year long "Joycean exile," at the end of which, as was the case with Horváth as well, came death in Paris. A further, external stimulus came from a recently published doctoral dissertation concerning history and fiction in Horváth's dramas (Jean-Claude François, *Histoire et fiction dans le théâtre d'Ödön von Horváth*, Presses Universitaires de Grenoble, 1978). On an unnumbered page of the manuscript of "The Stateless One," we find the following:

> A story about the *apatride* or the Man Without a Country has been an obsession of mine for years. Actually from the time I read a short note in a magazine about his life and his tragic end. At first I had in mind writing some kind of retrospective or scholarly study about him. I wrote down a few observations, some of those naïve notes in which you conceal your own thoughts behind your characters. That was all really just appeasing my conscience and the creation of an illusion that notes like that are the beginnings of stories, their nuclei, the load-bearing beams of a future prose construction. But of course I got no further than that. And then one day I came across (by accident?) a PhD thesis that dealt with my stateless man.

His character came back to life for me at once. And what did I find in this dissertation that related to my hero? A mass of useful information, dates, facts; but my story, my imaginary story atomized. The secret and mysterious atmosphere enveloping the life and death of my "hero" dissipated abruptly. But I nonetheless resolved to persevere, to try to bring back the atmosphere of secrets and the unknown. To write according to my own lights the bare-bones framework of facts, similar to a net of squares made of intersecting words.

(This passage, unchanged, could have formed part of a Postscript to *The Encyclopedia of the Dead*. It was probably written with that goal in mind.)

In manuscript form among Kiš's papers were preserved seven tables of contents of a book of stories that would be published in 1983 under the title *The Encyclopedia of the Dead*. The first two, which we can trace without difficulty to the year 1980, included the title "Ödön von Horváth," with a notation of the number of pages envisioned (ten in the first table of contents, and eight in the second). Both of the tables were written out by hand on half-sheets of typewriter paper. A remnant of cellophane tape attests to the fact that the list of titles (as if it were some literary duty) had been hung up in plain view somewhere. No tale involving Ödön von Horváth under any title, however, is to be found on the other five tables of contents, all of which were typed and which contain the titles of finished stories. We did, however, find forty-seven typed pages in Kiš's papers belonging to a "topic for a story" about the life and death of an *apatride*. One of them bears the title "APATRIDE/MAN WITHOUT A COUNTRY," typed in all capitals, and below that, in parentheses, "OUR HOMELAND IS THE MIND." We used the first, underlined word as the title of the story, regarding the other two titles as variants. Among the forty-seven mostly uncorrected pages, we were able to discern two entities; their relationship to each other was one of *first* and *second versions*. The first consists of fourteen numbered pages, with traces of corrections, apparently carried out in one sitting, with a fine-point black pen. The story of the stateless man, now bearing the name Egon von Németh (the exchange of the sur-name Horváth for Németh, aside from purely literary concerns, which lie outside the scope of these notes, is interesting in its own right: one common family name used to designate Hungarians living along the borders to Croatian areas has been traded for an equally common family name for Hungarians from border areas next to German-speaking territory), flows continuously in this version, without any kind of breaks, even among sections that are chronologically very far apart. In the text, however, there are fragments, designated by numbers and circled in the same black pen, that later, with almost no changes, appear in the second ver-sion of eight pages.

This second version comprises fifteen numbered sections. There is no title on the first page, something that could mean that this version served above all as an investigation of the suitability of the form: the fragment as a structural unit is being put to the test.

The question of structure is again of the greatest importance: the sequence of sections ("the texture of events"), their dimensions, the relationship between their relative lengths, interruption in the course of the narrative, and the nature of their graphic representations (characteristic here is the absence of long passages: every section has the semantic density of a stanza of poetry). At the top of the first and second sections there are, in addition, typed sentences taken word for word from scientific texts. A possible function of these quotes: the contribution to a sense of compression; but they have another, more important function: it is as if the author of *A Tomb for Boris Davidovich* wanted, through them, to say the following: "Look, ladies and gentlemen, what my starting point is, and look what it gives rise to, no matter how 'carefully' I exercise my 'creativity.'"

What about the contents of the remaining twenty-five pages? For the most part unpaginated, they are largely variants of the passages included in the two versions already mentioned. But there are those that show "first-hand" traces of events from the life of the *apatride* that encompass his entire history. We took it upon ourselves, not without trepidation, to piece the story together (the fragmentary character of the second version made our work easier). We found justification in our desire to defy the irreversible.

Textual Notes:

p. 15 *entirely vague and pointless*: Sentence incomplete.

p. 17 *And so forth*: A passage for which we could unfortunately find no place in the unified and recomposed "variant," given its similarity to this section/fragment, but could no more dispense with, on account of its function in the course of the narrative, is reproduced in its entirety here:

> Here, in Amsterdam, in an isolated street a stone's throw from a canal, our stateless man would suddenly find himself among his characters, a word that he used, not without attendant irony, every time his eye was drawn to those human creatures who bore on their faces or their bodies signs of rack and ruin, either patent or hidden. When night had begun its descent onto the streets, around the corner there would suddenly appear women, all dolled up, leaning against the wall in their tight, clingy dresses.

p. 18   *No more and no less so than other people. If he had been told this earlier, two or three years ago, he would not have paid any attention to it*: These two sentences were omitted from the first publication of the story (*Srpski književni glasnik*, 1, 1992).

Jurij Golec

In the last three of the seven tables of contents for *The Encyclopedia of the Dead*, the titles "Jurij Golec" and "The Lute and the Scars" both appear, in this order. In the seventh table of contents, both titles are crossed out by hand. Why were both removed, even though they dovetail with the basic theme of the book (both find their "metaphysical bearings" in love and death)? The reason (the only reason for which material evidence can be adduced) should perhaps be sought in the radical shift in style that comes from adjusting to their autobiographical, non-fictional character. In their stead "Red Stamps with Lenin's Picture" appeared at the last minute. We say "last minute" because the title of this other story is not found in any of the tables of contents, something that indicates that it was added to the manuscript just before it was turned over to the publisher. This piece of "fantasy" combines the worlds of the two stories while hewing more closely to the style of the whole *Encyclopedia*. Whether or not the inclusion of "Stamps" necessitated the exclusion of the other two stories for purely literary reasons is a question of another order, and one that does not lie within the scope of these notes.

The story "Jurij Golec" is preserved in manuscript form in four versions (not counting the layers of "palimpsests" created by revisions in the author's hand), totaling one hundred and nineteen typed pages, to which should be added fifty-five additional pieces of paper with variations on individual passages or notes and sketches. The sequence of the versions can be established with little difficulty. The first comprises twenty-six pages and has the title "The Actor"; the second, untitled version is forty pages long. Both of these versions contain only the first half of the story. The third version, and the fourth, definitive one, both bearing the title "Jurij Golec," are of almost equal length (27 and 26 pp.). The fundamental differences between the four versions are the visible reduction in text and the replacement of real personal names with fictitious names or initials. The basic technical issue, which is the main reason that multiple versions exist, is how to depict dialogue without narrative lulls or awkwardness. The customary forms "she said," "he said," or "I said," and so forth, are reduced to an absolute minimum (and in the final text are only used when needed for rhythm or comprehension). The basic events, characters, and situations, however, remained unchanged.

In view of the fact that this story was planned to be a part of *The Encyclopedia of the Dead*, Kiš wrote a note that was supposed to be included in a general postscript, which we have appended to the story in this volume, rather than place here among the notes. It was our view that the subsequent revelation of the hero's identity retrospectively underscored the nonfictional nature of the story, whereas the typical novelistic feature of a "note" would broaden to too great a degree the world of the basic narrative. In terms of form, we find this is justified by the fact that the story "The Short Biography of A.A. Darmolatov" (in *A Tomb for Boris Davidovich*) concludes with an italicized postscript.

The Lute and the Scars

"The Lute and the Scars" was also conceived as part of *The Encyclopedia of the Dead*. We have already made mention (see previous note) of some of our hypotheses about the reasons this story, as was the case with "Jurij Golec," did not make it into the collection. Two versions are preserved in manuscript form: the first, without a title, contains seventeen typed pages (fifteen of which are sequentially paginated, though among them are inserted two pages with the designations "2a" and "6a"); the second, entitled "The Lute and the Scars," consists of fourteen unfilled pages. Versions of the introductory section of the story make up most of the content of another sixteen pages. And, again, it is to the story itself that we attached the "note" that was foreseen as a general postscript. In this case we acted with much greater hesitation than with "Jurij Golec." The reasons were that this note has primarily a theoretical and meta-textual function: it specifies the genre (creative nonfiction), with an additional reference to the story "Jurij Golec." The gulf between Kiš's narration and his commentary is much wider here. The fact is, however, that the word "note" itself seems intended to strengthen, even to guarantee, the truthfulness of the story (even, if nothing else, by comparison with the foregoing story, in which the inclusion of the fictional was a kind of obligation).

Let us now shift our attention to the thematic uniqueness of this story in the context of Kiš's literary oeuvre: this is the only piece that one could label a "Belgrade story." The piece was written at the start of 1983, as a late look back at his own younger years, with a double distancing from the objects he is describing: in terms of space, since at that time Kiš was living in Paris, and likewise at a chronological remove (the story takes place during the 1950s, with one episode from the end of the 1960s). Everything in the piece is tied up with a quintessential story of emigration, the roots of which reach back to the Russian Revolution. And it is precisely this aspect of the story that links it, along with "The Book of Kings and Fools" (from *The Encyclopedia of the Dead*), to the world of *A Tomb for Boris Davidovich*. The reference to *The Protocols of the Elders of Zion* is not simply part and parcel of Kiš's memories of his youth (and an indirect reference to two treatments of the subject that Kiš penned much earlier, both published in the newspaper *Ovdje* (Here): "On Céline" from April 1971 and "Anti-Semitism as a Way of Looking at the World" from June of the same year), but also a representation of the subtle affinities between these two stories. (For example, the profession of the hero of "The Book of Kings and Fools," Belogortsev—a forestry engineer—along with a few other details that the attentive reader will unearth.)

The Poet

Although the title "The Poet" is not mentioned in any of the tables of contents for *The Encyclopedia of the Dead*, one handwritten fragment, found among texts that can with certainty be linked to that book, shows us to be justified in placing the story into this context. This is the fragment:

> A story about a professor who writes a
>   sonnet against Tito and the Party.
> After years of a sentence of hard labor,
>   this sonnet has been reworked into
>   a paean.
> They bring Ranković to see him, etc.

Two sonnets.

On the back of one page of notes to "Jurij Golec" we find the following written by hand:

> For the story:
> 1. The mayor destroys the park.
> 2. *Sonnet* (of a reactionary)

The manuscript of "The Poet" consists of thirteen continuously paginated typed pages. Corrections were made in three rounds: with a pencil and with fine blue and black ballpoint pens. There are no other related papers: the story came into existence in one sitting, with only superficial changes.

The appearance of this story among Kiš's short fiction is not, however, accidental. Traces of his reflections on the postwar years are to be seen in his notes, in his sketches of imaginative literary subjects, and in fragmentary autobiographical notes relating to the Cetinje period of the author's life. From among the large number of such notes we will reproduce here a few that correspond to this story:

> "[P]arty spirit" in literature; the revolution isn't for young ladies; terror in school: tight pants ("knickerbockers"), haircut, etc. . . . morale; Lenin-Stalin in physics, history, math, etc; language: the manner of speech of politicians and peasants; warehouses belonging to government ministries.

In addition, we include a short character sketch:

> Cetinje: secret policeman/tennis player: he has an odd
> way of walking, not peasantlike, or clumsy, not at all, but
> rather a gait that you couldn't help but watch (even though
> a gait cannot be viewed or seen): it was, how shall I say,
> the walk of a peasant who is walking as if he were middle
> class, *who thinks he is walking as if he were a middle-class*
> *person who plays tennis.*

Subsequent to the first publication of this story in the initial edition of the collection *The Lute and the Scars,* we found amid some newspaper clippings a bundle of Kiš's papers that contained several relevant items, including a bibliography that the author undoubtedly composed in the course of preparing his collected works. On one sheet from this bundle we found the following note that indicates the "sources" of this story, its nonfictional background:

> People told me a story about a man somewhere who was
> arrested after the war on account of some subversive po-
> etry. They threw him into prison and forgot about him.
> Then someone remembered he was there and ordered
> him the opportunity to clean up the mess himself: in
> place of his subversive poem (semiliterate slapdash work)
> he must write a poem with the opposite content. The man
> accepted the offer. They gave him a distant, very distant
> deadline, provided him with paper and a pencil: and said

write, and erase, until it is first-rate. From time to time they summoned him and he read aloud his panegyric. "It could be better, *more sincere!*" they told him. People from the most prominent circles of the police force visited him and read through his variations. After ten years someone told him: "Well, see, now it is first-rate. The poem is sincere." And—they let him go.

(So much for needing to research the relationship between an anecdote and a piece of fiction . . .)

The Debt

The story "The Debt" is preserved among Kiš's manuscript papers on a total of seventeen typewritten pages. The complete manuscript of the version we provide here contains twelve numbered pages; in the middle of the first is the typed title "The Debt." Four of the additional pages present what is in all likelihood a second version of the beginning of the story, in this case with no title indicated. On a separate page, on which the title is also to be found, there are simply five lines, which can be regarded as another variant of the start of the story.

Corrections on the twelve-page manuscript were carried out with a pencil throughout the entire text, with the majority of these occurring in the introductory section that precedes the enumeration of the "debts." These corrections, judging by their apparent uniformity, were carried out in a single reading of the manuscript.

The other corrections, decidedly fewer in number, were made in fine blue ballpoint pen (the story therefore seems most likely to have gone through only two revisions). The unfinished nature of certain sentences, which we encounter from the first pages of the story, along with superficial corrections that seem to be "final touches"—these all demonstrate that Kiš's opinion of the introductory section was that it was only a temporary resolution. In the portion of the story where the enumerations occur, there are virtually no corrections of any kind, which shows that the frame-narrative was what caused the most problems for Kiš; once the list begins, the only narrative events are those concerned with the debts, and the underlying concept that life is passing before the protagonist's eyes by means of this inventory, all of which was drafted without the least difficulty or deficiency (the process of enumeration that was so dear to Kiš). To judge by the large number of sentences beginning on one page and concluding on the next, we could even say that the story was produced in one session.

The title "The Debt" does not figure in any of the seven extant tables of contents for *The Encyclopedia of the Dead*, which would seem to indicate that the story was written after 1983. The reader will probably recognize the great Bosnian author Ivo Andrić in the character of "the debtor." And this identification, among other things, leads us to take 1986 as the year of origin for the story: at that time Kiš was writing the foreword to the French edition of Andrić's *The Woman from Sarajevo*. Although arising in connection with this special occasion, Kiš's repeated focus on Andrić could also have been the stimulus for the production of this type of homage to that other writer, one of the closest relatives in Kiš's "literary family tree." Even the fact that the story remained unfinished validates our view that its genesis should be associated with the aforementioned year, before the end of which Kiš's illness had manifested itself.

Nearly all the persons mentioned in this story are connected with Andrić's early life (his schooling, his start as a writer, his first years in the diplomatic service) and Kiš located information about them in Miroslav Karaulac's book *Rani Andrić* (The Early Andrić, Prosveta/Svjetlost, 1980), which he even mentions right at the beginning of the French foreword. Singling them out from the abundance of persons who come up in Karaulac's study, he transformed them into character-paradigms via a process of extreme fictional compression, that essential hallmark of his prose. "Andrić is undoubtedly a moralist," Kiš would go on to write, assessing the former's literary works ("A Foreword to *The Woman from Sarajevo*," in *Život, literatura*, Svjetlost, 1990); thus both his selection of facts and his formulation of statements (often in the form of maxims) are made according to principles that might be ascribed to a writer-moralist. The story, however, functions as a double portrait (the portrait and the vase), for Kiš is also taking moral stock of his own experiences and inclinations (the delicate terrain of good deeds and gratitude). And we believe that readers will have an easy time identifying points of contact between the characters in this "double exposition." (The last will and testament of Eugène Ionesco, published in *Le Figaro littéraire* after that writer's death, was written in the form of a life reviewed as a balance sheet of debts; when compared with the story "The Debt," which was written nearly a decade earlier, Ionesco's will can serve as evidence that even literature knows something about wondrous coincidences and the affinities of kinship.)

Textual Notes:

p. 83   *They served as a kind of rosary*: The following sentences
were crossed out: "He needed to distribute his two hundred crowns fairly, the amount his stipend brought him,
and not remain in debt to anyone. Because at this moment he knew, with the lucidity that comes with the hour
before death [. . .]."

p. 83   *The idea came to him, struck a part of his consciousness*:
This seems to bear little direct connection to what pre-
ceded it, even considering the cancelled lines mentioned
above. It's difficult to say why this gap emerged, though
the reasons for the deletion of the missing sentences are
clear enough: the prematurely delivered exposition and
the stylistic rawness of the second, unfinished sentence.

p. 84   . . . *it made him chuckle to himself*: Left out of the first
publication (*Književne novine*, October 15, 1992).

p. 84   *for all human endeavors . . . in silence*: From Andrić's letter to
Tugomir Alaupović of July 6, 1920. Cited in Miroslav Karaulac, *Rani Andrić* (Beograd: Prosveta, 1980), 154–55.

p. 84   *over the course of his life*: Written by hand on the margin
was this (possible) addition to the sentence: "Jelena, for
instance (and he tossed the thought away as from the

deck of a ship . . . for it was too painful)."

p. 84   *the eyes of posterity*: Written in pencil in the margin and on the back of the third page of the manuscript. In the text itself, following the colon (". . . in bundles: poems, journals, notes . . ."), is a section that is circled in pencil and that contains only incomplete sentences. The circling might be understood as the designation of the spot to which the text from the margin and back of the page should be inserted (possibly as a substitution). This allows us to replace the incomplete passage from the main text and preserve it here. It reads: "love letters that, wrapped in the old-fashioned way with purple ribbon, he kept his whole life (and in which was . . .) politically compromising . . . A will written down . . ."

p. 85   *proving a fool to be a fool amounts to compromising oneself*: Incomplete.

p. 85   *As for the spiritual debts . . . one's homeland*: The material in this paragraph up to this sentence was crossed out by two heavy diagonal lines. However, since the text that follows represents a natural continuation of what was crossed out, and cannot be understood without it, we decided not to move it to a note.

p. 86   *two crowns*: The amount of the debt was written in by hand, later, first spelled out (*"dvije krune"*) and then with a digit. Considering the second method to be temporary, and chosen by the author for simplicity's sake, we have written out all numbers in this story.

p. 89 . . . *historical necessity*: A portion of this sentence, somewhat altered, comes from the story "Dogs and Books" in *A Tomb for Boris Davidovich*.

p. 89 *To Count Ivo Vojnović*: This was proceeded in the manuscript by an incomplete entry: "To Mrs. Zdenka Marković . . ."

p. 90 *Mrs. Vera Stojić*: Andrić's girlfriend from wartime bohemian circles in Zagreb, with whom the writer carried on a lively correspondence during his stay in Rome in the early 1920s. In one of these letters we find the following sentence, which could as well have been written by Kiš: "I write little, and with difficulty; nothing exists without our country; and I can live neither with it nor without it." Karaulac's book contains, however, no information at all about the character of Mrs. Stojić, who was obviously Andrić's privileged interlocutor, which perhaps accounts for the brevity of her entry here.

A and B

We can date this short piece of prose with relative certainty to 1986, the year that Kiš's illness was diagnosed; the work has no title and consists of two circled entries labeled "A" and "B," each of which has a subtitle in English: *The magical place* and *The worst rathole I visited?* This text, comprising three typed pages, was found in Kiš's literary papers already prepared for publication, with the author's name in the upper left-hand corner of the first page. Aside from the issue of dating the text, we were vexed by the question of why Kiš would suddenly return to themes, places (which are here placed in sharp opposition to each other, as indicated by the titles of the constituent parts: magical place and worst rat-hole), and images from his "family cycle"; and we were inclined, trusting in the correctness of our intuition, to link this "homesickness" with forebodings of his own imminent end. Today, following closer studies of his literary oeuvre, and an inventory of its topics and motifs, made over nearly an entire decade (from 1978 to 1986), we realize that our assumption was more a matter of the "treacherous influence of biography."

(Mme Pascal Delpeche recently mentioned to us that this text could be a response to a questionnaire about "most beautiful and ugliest places" received by the author. While this solution would remove all mystification as to Kiš's motive, it would not alter the significance of the chosen places themselves.)

The Marathon Runner and the Race Official

The story "The Marathon Runner and the Race Official" was written in Belgrade in the summer of 1982. It was intended for the volume *The Encyclopedia of the Dead*, as attested by the fact that the title is mentioned in the first three tables of contents for that work. The manuscript includes six continuously paginated typed pages. In Kiš's papers, however, we found only the second, third, fourth, and fifth. Due to the fragmentary nature of the text, which we considered final, we did not publish the story in the first edition of *The Lute and the Scars*. It was, together with other fragmentary texts, published in the book *Skladište*, which contains all of Kiš's unpublished literary papers. A few days after that book appeared, as we were completing work on a bibliography (the date was March 4, 1995), we leafed through a number of folders of press clippings. In the first folder we picked up, we noticed, between two yellowed sheets of newspaper, the missing pages (pp. 1 and 6) for which we had been searching in vain for two years. We revel in this miracle, which needs no commentary!

On two other pages were found additional elements intended for the story, which ostensibly should have formed part of its postscript. It is a matter of a brief introductory comment and also the translation of an anecdote from Abram Tertz's book *A Voice from the Chorus*, which formed the basis of the story. We reproduce both of them here in this summary annotation:

> (At one time I thought that it would be interesting to include in *The Encyclopedia of the Dead* the following text by Tertz as an appendix, in the manner of a Borgesian *et cetera*.)
>
> "Someone told us about a dream seen by a Latvian serving a 25-year sentence. In the dim and distant past,

he had been an athlete, and he dreamed he was a young man again, taking part in a 25-kilometre marathon race. He had a feeling of great physical well-being, almost of intoxication. But just as he had run half the course, the umpire suddenly appeared out of the blue: "Enough! It's time you took a rest." The Latvian tried to refuse, saying he wasn't a bit tired. The umpire gently but firmly insisted: "Take a rest!" His late wife was there too, and she joined in, saying: "That will do! Enough!" Next morning the former runner had no sooner told his dream to his friends than he dropped dead of heart failure. He had precisely 12 years and 6 months to go before the end of his sentence." [from Kyril Fitzlyon's and Max Hayward's excellent translation of Tertz's *A Voice from the Chorus*. (New York: Farrar, Straus, and Giroux, 1976), p. 75.]

Leonid Šejka died in November, 1970.

TRANSLATOR'S NOTES

A and B

The italicized phrases in this piece are in English in the original text. Additionally, the parenthetical statement in the first paragraph was originally written in French.

The Marathon Runner and the Race Official

p. 99   *on the sidewalks* . . . : The available Serbo-Croatian text of this story picks up here, after the word "sidewalks." It runs for most of the story, up to the sentence ending ". . . for more than fifteen years." (See the following note). This text is found in the section labeled "FRAGMENTI" in the compendium *"Dosije Enciklopedija mrtvih,"* in Mirjana Miočinović, ed., *Skladište* (Beograd: BIGZ, 1995), 336–40. The first and last sections of this story were translated from the French and German versions published after the missing pages of Kiš's manuscript were found. These works are: *Le luth et les cicatrices*, translated by Pascale Delpech (Paris: Fayard, 1995) and *Der Heimatlose: Erzählungen*, translated by Ilma Rakusa (München: Carl Hanser Verlag, 1996).

p. 105   *for more than fifteen years*: This phrase marks the end of the Serbo-Croatian text available for first publication in 1995.

DANILO KIŠ was one of Serbia's most influential writers and the author of several novels and short-story collections, including *A Tomb for Boris Davidovich*, *Hourglass*, and *Garden, Ashes*. He died in 1989 at the age of 54.

JOHN K. COX is professor of history and department head at North Dakota State University. His translations include the novel *The Attic* by Danilo Kiš, as well as short fiction by Kiš, Ismail Kadare, Ivan Ivanji, Ivo Andrić, and Meša Selimović.

SELECTED DALKEY ARCHIVE TITLES

PETROS ABATZOGLOU, *What Does Mrs. Freeman Want?*
MICHAL AJVAZ, *The Golden Age.*
The Other City.
PIERRE ALBERT-BIROT, *Grabinoulor.*
YUZ ALESHKOVSKY, *Kangaroo.*
FELIPE ALFAU, *Chromos.*
Locos.
JOÃO ALMINO, *The Book of Emotions.*
IVAN ÂNGELO, *The Celebration.*
The Tower of Glass.
DAVID ANTIN, *Talking.*
ANTÓNIO LOBO ANTUNES, *Knowledge of Hell.*
The Splendor of Portugal.
ALAIN ARIAS-MISSON, *Theatre of Incest.*
IFTIKHAR ARIF AND WAQAS KHWAJA, EDS., *Modern Poetry of Pakistan.*
JOHN ASHBERY AND JAMES SCHUYLER, *A Nest of Ninnies.*
ROBERT ASHLEY, *Perfect Lives.*
GABRIELA AVIGUR-ROTEM, *Heatwave and Crazy Birds.*
HEIMRAD BÄCKER, *transcript.*
DJUNA BARNES, *Ladies Almanack.*
Ryder.
JOHN BARTH, *LETTERS.*
Sabbatical.
DONALD BARTHELME, *The King.*
Paradise.
SVETISLAV BASARA, *Chinese Letter.*
MIQUEL BAUÇÀ, *The Siege in the Room.*
RENÉ BELLETTO, *Dying.*
MAREK BIEŃCZYK, *Transparency.*
MARK BINELLI, *Sacco and Vanzetti Must Die!*
ANDREI BITOV, *Pushkin House.*
ANDREJ BLATNIK, *You Do Understand.*
LOUIS PAUL BOON, *Chapel Road.*
My Little War.
Summer in Termuren.
ROGER BOYLAN, *Killoyle.*
IGNÁCIO DE LOYOLA BRANDÃO, *Anonymous Celebrity.*
The Good-Bye Angel.
Teeth under the Sun.
Zero.
BONNIE BREMSER, *Troia: Mexican Memoirs.*
CHRISTINE BROOKE-ROSE, *Amalgamemnon.*
BRIGID BROPHY, *In Transit.*
MEREDITH BROSNAN, *Mr. Dynamite.*
GERALD L. BRUNS, *Modern Poetry and the Idea of Language.*
EVGENY BUNIMOVICH AND J. KATES, EDS., *Contemporary Russian Poetry: An Anthology.*
GABRIELLE BURTON, *Heartbreak Hotel.*
MICHEL BUTOR, *Degrees.*
Mobile.
Portrait of the Artist as a Young Ape.
G. CABRERA INFANTE, *Infante's Inferno.*
Three Trapped Tigers.
JULIETA CAMPOS, *The Fear of Losing Eurydice.*
ANNE CARSON, *Eros the Bittersweet.*
ORLY CASTEL-BLOOM, *Dolly City.*
CAMILO JOSÉ CELA, *Christ versus Arizona.*
The Family of Pascual Duarte.
The Hive.
LOUIS-FERDINAND CÉLINE, *Castle to Castle.*
Conversations with Professor Y.
London Bridge.

Normance.
North.
Rigadoon.
MARIE CHAIX, *The Laurels of Lake Constance.*
HUGO CHARTERIS, *The Tide Is Right.*
JEROME CHARYN, *The Tar Baby.*
ERIC CHEVILLARD, *Demolishing Nisard.*
LUIS CHITARRONI, *The No Variations.*
MARC CHOLODENKO, *Mordechai Schamz.*
JOSHUA COHEN, *Witz.*
EMILY HOLMES COLEMAN, *The Shutter of Snow.*
ROBERT COOVER, *A Night at the Movies.*
STANLEY CRAWFORD, *Log of the S.S. The Mrs Unguentine.*
Some Instructions to My Wife.
ROBERT CREELEY, *Collected Prose.*
RENÉ CREVEL, *Putting My Foot in It.*
RALPH CUSACK, *Cadenza.*
SUSAN DAITCH, *L.C.*
Storytown.
NICHOLAS DELBANCO, *The Count of Concord.*
Sherbrookes.
NIGEL DENNIS, *Cards of Identity.*
PETER DIMOCK, *A Short Rhetoric for Leaving the Family.*
ARIEL DORFMAN, *Konfidenz.*
COLEMAN DOWELL, *The Houses of Children.*
Island People.
Too Much Flesh and Jabez.
ARKADII DRAGOMOSHCHENKO, *Dust.*
RIKKI DUCORNET, *The Complete Butcher's Tales.*
The Fountains of Neptune.
The Jade Cabinet.
The One Marvelous Thing.
Phosphor in Dreamland.
The Stain.
The Word "Desire."
WILLIAM EASTLAKE, *The Bamboo Bed.*
Castle Keep.
Lyric of the Circle Heart.
JEAN ECHENOZ, *Chopin's Move.*
STANLEY ELKIN, *A Bad Man.*
Boswell: A Modern Comedy.
Criers and Kibitzers, Kibitzers and Criers.
The Dick Gibson Show.
The Franchiser.
George Mills.
The Living End.
The MacGuffin.
The Magic Kingdom.
Mrs. Ted Bliss.
The Rabbi of Lud.
Van Gogh's Room at Arles.
FRANÇOIS EMMANUEL, *Invitation to a Voyage.*
ANNIE ERNAUX, *Cleaned Out.*
SALVADOR ESPRIU, *Ariadne in the Grotesque Labyrinth.*
LAUREN FAIRBANKS, *Muzzle Thyself.*
Sister Carrie.
LESLIE A. FIEDLER, *Love and Death in the American Novel.*
JUAN FILLOY, *Faction.*
Op Oloop.
ANDY FITCH, *Pop Poetics.*
GUSTAVE FLAUBERT, *Bouvard and Pécuchet.*
KASS FLEISHER, *Talking out of School.*

FOR A FULL LIST OF PUBLICATIONS, VISIT:
www.dalkeyarchive.com

FORD MADOX FORD,
The March of Literature.
JON FOSSE, *Aliss at the Fire.*
Melancholy.
MAX FRISCH, *I'm Not Stiller.*
Man in the Holocene.
CARLOS FUENTES, *Christopher Unborn.*
Distant Relations.
Terra Nostra.
Vlad.
Where the Air Is Clear.
TAKEHIKO FUKUNAGA, *Flowers of Grass.*
WILLIAM GADDIS, *J R.*
The Recognitions.
JANICE GALLOWAY, *Foreign Parts.*
The Trick Is to Keep Breathing.
WILLIAM H. GASS, *Cartesian Sonata*
and Other Novellas.
Finding a Form.
A Temple of Texts.
The Tunnel.
Willie Masters' Lonesome Wife.
GÉRARD GAVARRY, *Hoppla! 1 2 3.*
Making a Novel.
ETIENNE GILSON,
The Arts of the Beautiful.
Forms and Substances in the Arts.
C. S. GISCOMBE, *Giscome Road.*
Here.
Prairie Style.
DOUGLAS GLOVER, *Bad News of the Heart.*
The Enamoured Knight.
WITOLD GOMBROWICZ,
A Kind of Testament.
PAULO EMÍLIO SALES GOMES, *P's Three*
Women.
KAREN ELIZABETH GORDON, *The Red Shoes.*
GEORGI GOSPODINOV, *Natural Novel.*
JUAN GOYTISOLO, *Count Julian.*
Exiled from Almost Everywhere.
Juan the Landless.
Makbara.
Marks of Identity.
PATRICK GRAINVILLE, *The Cave of Heaven.*
HENRY GREEN, *Back.*
Blindness.
Concluding.
Doting.
Nothing.
JACK GREEN, *Fire the Bastards!*
JIŘÍ GRUŠA, *The Questionnaire.*
GABRIEL GUDDING,
Rhode Island Notebook.
MELA HARTWIG, *Am I a Redundant*
Human Being?
JOHN HAWKES, *The Passion Artist.*
Whistlejacket.
ELIZABETH HEIGHWAY, ED., *Contemporary*
Georgian Fiction.
ALEKSANDAR HEMON, ED.,
Best European Fiction.
AIDAN HIGGINS, *Balcony of Europe.*
A Bestiary.
Blind Man's Bluff
Bornholm Night-Ferry.
Darkling Plain: Texts for the Air.
Flotsam and Jetsam.
Langrishe, Go Down.
Scenes from a Receding Past.
Windy Arbours.
KEIZO HINO, *Isle of Dreams.*
KAZUSHI HOSAKA, *Plainsong.*

ALDOUS HUXLEY, *Antic Hay.*
Crome Yellow.
Point Counter Point.
Those Barren Leaves.
Time Must Have a Stop.
NAOYUKI II, *The Shadow of a Blue Cat.*
MIKHAIL IOSSEL AND JEFF PARKER, EDS.,
Amerika: Russian Writers View the
United States.
DRAGO JANČAR, *The Galley Slave.*
GERT JONKE, *The Distant Sound.*
Geometric Regional Novel.
Homage to Czerny.
The System of Vienna.
JACQUES JOUET, *Mountain R.*
Savage.
Upstaged.
CHARLES JULIET, *Conversations with*
Samuel Beckett and Bram van
Velde.
MIEKO KANAI, *The Word Book.*
YORAM KANIUK, *Life on Sandpaper.*
HUGH KENNER, *The Counterfeiters.*
Flaubert, Joyce and Beckett:
The Stoic Comedians.
Joyce's Voices.
DANILO KIŠ, *The Attic.*
Garden, Ashes.
The Lute and the Scars
Psalm 44.
A Tomb for Boris Davidovich.
ANITA KONKKA, *A Fool's Paradise.*
GEORGE KONRÁD, *The City Builder.*
TADEUSZ KONWICKI, *A Minor Apocalypse.*
The Polish Complex.
MENIS KOUMANDAREAS, *Koula.*
ELAINE KRAF, *The Princess of 72nd Street.*
JIM KRUSOE, *Iceland.*
AYŞE KULIN, *Farewell: A Mansion in*
Occupied Istanbul.
EWA KURYLUK, *Century 21.*
EMILIO LASCANO TEGUI, *On Elegance*
While Sleeping.
ERIC LAURRENT, *Do Not Touch.*
HERVÉ LE TELLIER, *The Sextine Chapel.*
A Thousand Pearls (for a Thousand
Pennies)
VIOLETTE LEDUC, *La Bâtarde.*
EDOUARD LEVÉ, *Autoportrait.*
Suicide.
MARIO LEVI, *Istanbul Was a Fairy Tale.*
SUZANNE JILL LEVINE, *The Subversive*
Scribe: Translating Latin
American Fiction.
DEBORAH LEVY, *Billy and Girl.*
Pillow Talk in Europe and Other
Places.
JOSÉ LEZAMA LIMA, *Paradiso.*
ROSA LIKSOM, *Dark Paradise.*
OSMAN LINS, *Avalovara.*
The Queen of the Prisons of Greece.
ALF MAC LOCHLAINN,
The Corpus in the Library.
Out of Focus.
RON LOEWINSOHN, *Magnetic Field(s).*
MINA LOY, *Stories and Essays of Mina Loy.*
BRIAN LYNCH, *The Winner of Sorrow.*
D. KEITH MANO, *Take Five.*
MICHELINE AHARONIAN MARCOM,
The Mirror in the Well.
BEN MARCUS,
The Age of Wire and String.

SELECTED DALKEY ARCHIVE TITLES

WALLACE MARKFIELD,
Teitlebaum's Window.
To an Early Grave.
DAVID MARKSON, *Reader's Block.*
Springer's Progress.
Wittgenstein's Mistress.
CAROLE MASO, *AVA.*
LADISLAV MATEJKA AND KRYSTYNA
POMORSKA, EDS.,
Readings in Russian Poetics:
Formalist and Structuralist Views.
HARRY MATHEWS,
The Case of the Persevering Maltese:
Collected Essays.
Cigarettes.
The Conversions.
The Human Country: New and
Collected Stories.
The Journalist.
My Life in CIA.
Singular Pleasures.
The Sinking of the Odradek
Stadium.
Tlooth.
20 Lines a Day.
JOSEPH MCELROY,
Night Soul and Other Stories.
THOMAS MCGONIGLE,
Going to Patchogue.
ROBERT L. MCLAUGHLIN, ED., *Innovations:*
An Anthology of Modern &
Contemporary Fiction.
ABDELWAHAB MEDDEB, *Talismano.*
GERHARD MEIER, *Isle of the Dead.*
HERMAN MELVILLE, *The Confidence-Man.*
AMANDA MICHALOPOULOU, *I'd Like.*
STEVEN MILLHAUSER, *The Barnum Museum.*
In the Penny Arcade.
RALPH J. MILLS, JR., *Essays on Poetry.*
MOMUS, *The Book of Jokes.*
CHRISTINE MONTALBETTI, *The Origin of Man.*
Western.
OLIVE MOORE, *Spleen.*
NICHOLAS MOSLEY, *Accident.*
Assassins.
Catastrophe Practice.
Children of Darkness and Light.
Experience and Religion.
A Garden of Trees.
God's Hazard.
The Hesperides Tree.
Hopeful Monsters.
Imago Bird.
Impossible Object.
Inventing God.
Judith.
Look at the Dark.
Natalie Natalia.
Paradoxes of Peace.
Serpent.
Time at War.
The Uses of Slime Mould:
Essays of Four Decades.
WARREN MOTTE,
Fables of the Novel: French Fiction
since 1990.
Fiction Now: The French Novel in
the 21st Century.
Oulipo: A Primer of Potential
Literature.
GERALD MURNANE, *Barley Patch.*
Inland.

YVES NAVARRE, *Our Share of Time.*
Sweet Tooth.
DOROTHY NELSON, *In Night's City.*
Tar and Feathers.
ESHKOL NEVO, *Homesick.*
WILFRIDO D. NOLLEDO, *But for the Lovers.*
FLANN O'BRIEN, *At Swim-Two-Birds.*
At War.
The Best of Myles.
The Dalkey Archive.
Further Cuttings.
The Hard Life.
The Poor Mouth.
The Third Policeman.
CLAUDE OLLIER, *The Mise-en-Scène.*
Wert and the Life Without End.
GIOVANNI ORELLI, *Walaschek's Dream.*
PATRIK OUŘEDNÍK, *Europeana.*
The Opportune Moment, 1855.
BORIS PAHOR, *Necropolis.*
FERNANDO DEL PASO, *News from the Empire.*
Palinuro of Mexico.
ROBERT PINGET, *The Inquisitory.*
Mahu or The Material.
Trio.
A. G. PORTA, *The No World Concerto.*
MANUEL PUIG, *Betrayed by Rita Hayworth.*
The Buenos Aires Affair.
Heartbreak Tango.
RAYMOND QUENEAU, *The Last Days.*
Odile.
Pierrot Mon Ami.
Saint Glinglin.
ANN QUIN, *Berg.*
Passages.
Three.
Tripticks.
ISHMAEL REED, *The Free-Lance Pallbearers.*
The Last Days of Louisiana Red.
Ishmael Reed: The Plays.
Juice!
Reckless Eyeballing.
The Terrible Threes.
The Terrible Twos.
Yellow Back Radio Broke-Down.
JASIA REICHARDT, *15 Journeys Warsaw*
to London.
NOËLLE REVAZ, *With the Animals.*
JOÃO UBALDO RIBEIRO, *House of the*
Fortunate Buddhas.
JEAN RICARDOU, *Place Names.*
RAINER MARIA RILKE, *The Notebooks of*
Malte Laurids Brigge.
JULIÁN RÍOS, *The House of Ulysses.*
Larva: A Midsummer Night's Babel.
Poundemonium.
Procession of Shadows.
AUGUSTO ROA BASTOS, *I the Supreme.*
DANIËL ROBBERECHTS, *Arriving in Avignon.*
JEAN ROLIN, *The Explosion of the*
Radiator Hose.
OLIVIER ROLIN, *Hotel Crystal.*
ALIX CLEO ROUBAUD, *Alix's Journal.*
JACQUES ROUBAUD, *The Form of a*
City Changes Faster, Alas, Than
the Human Heart.
The Great Fire of London.
Hortense in Exile.
Hortense Is Abducted.
The Loop.
Mathematics:
The Plurality of Worlds of Lewis.

SELECTED DALKEY ARCHIVE TITLES

FOR A FULL LIST OF PUBLICATIONS, VISIT:
www.dalkeyarchive.com